FOREVER
AND A DAY

O.L. Obonna

First Published in Great Britain in 2021 by
LOVE AFRICA PRESS
103 Reaver House, 12 East Street, Epsom KT17 1HX
www.loveafricapress.com

LOVE AFRICA
PRESS
African Love Stories

BLURB

Their forbidden night leads to an inescapable consequence!

Her mind-blowing encounter with a handsome stranger rocked her to the core! It was a night she would never forget. Then Mma Nwachukwu discovers that the compelling stranger she lost her virginity to was none other than Fuad Danjuma, the younger brother of her new boss! Mma is stunned, especially when she discovers the thrilling and unforgettable night has left them bound for life.

When Fuad finds out Mma is pregnant, he is determined to do the right thing and claim her as his wife. Unfortunately, he offers her everything except the one thing she wants the most: his heart.

The trouble is, Mma is determined to wed for love.

PROLOGUE

In less than twenty-four hours, Mma Nwachukwu would become Mrs Mma Danjuma.

Today was her wedding day, and it was meant to be the happiest day of her life.

Scratch that. It was meant to be the happiest day in any woman's life.

Not in Mma's case.

Her eyes filled with tears, and she hurriedly swiped her cheeks. She didn't want anyone walking in and seeing her tears.

That wouldn't do at all. Everybody thought it was love at first sight for her and Fuad, but she accepted the truth. Fuad did too. More moisture clouded her vision, and she buried her face in her hands.

She was the envy of all her friends. She, a nobody, was marrying Fuad Danjuma, the heir to the Danjuma fortune. Drop-dead gorgeous and wealthy to boot, Fuad was supposed to be every woman's dream, but he was not hers.

Mma shook her head as the tears ran down her cheeks and seeped through her fingers.

She had been so stupid. It was all her fault. This wasn't the life she wanted, stuck in a marriage to a man marrying her out of duty. Even though he was an amazing man, caring and decent, this was not a love marriage.

What was it he said the night he told her they would get married?

"Deal with it, Mma. Tomorrow we will see Aunty Ekene and my mum, she flew into Lagos today from Kano. We might not be getting married for love, but we are definitely getting married, and it is going to be a real marriage in every sense of the word."

No, this wasn't the life she wanted for herself. But, in less than twenty-four hours, she would be Mrs Mma Danjuma.

CHAPTER ONE

Three months ago

"Mma, your mother is going to be upset," Aunty Ekene said, handing her niece a drink before taking a seat opposite her. "She will blame me as usual."

"I know," Mma replied quietly.

Mum would not be happy that Mma went to her aunt for help. But she had no other choice. Things had deteriorated. Mma was at her wit's end. She couldn't continue like this, living from hand to mouth.

Life had always been challenging for them. Her father had died when Mma was ten years old, leaving her mother with three children. Nevertheless, Mma had managed to finish university with Aunty Ekene's help, against her mother's wishes.

Mma smiled at her Aunty Ekene, who looked so much like her mother, albeit a younger and petite version. In her early 40s, her aunt was small and pretty with unusually long hair, permanently worn as cornrows. She was an advocate for natural hair and was very stylish with it.

Mma couldn't understand her mother's anger towards her sister. Mum regularly grumbled about how Aunty Ekene had thrown away her values and married for money and how her husband was hobnobbing with corrupt Nigerian politicians.

Her aunt and her husband, Uncle Lotanna, had a beautiful relationship. He adored his wife, who in turn worshipped the ground her husband walked on. From day one, when Uncle Lotanna had stepped into their house, he had offered to help Mum with her children's education. Her mother had politely refused. When it was time for Mma to go to university, she ignored her mother and turned to her aunt for help.

Now a graduate, Mma had been at home for two years, no job. And her mother had forbidden her from reaching out to her aunt. But she was done listening to her mother. Her younger sisters were at home because they could not pay their school fees. So, two nights ago, she'd had a heated conversation with Mum and had walked out of the house. She needed a job and fast too, so she had gone straight to her aunt's house.

"Aunty, what do you want me to do?" Mma asked, shoulders stooped. "Kelechi and Kaira are home. I don't have a job. We can barely feed! I must have dropped my CV in a million places. No luck with that." She shook her head, "Please, Aunty, I need your help."

"Mma, it's not an issue. I just wish your mum would accept my support. Why is she so proud? She says Lotanna is not a decent person. I don't know how else to explain to her that Lotanna is a good person. The fact that he has friends who are politicians does not make him corrupt. So why on earth would she even think it?"

"I have no idea. Aunty, please, what can you do to help me. Please, I am desperate here."

Mma twisted her hands on her laps, blinking and trying hard not to cry. Aunt Ekene reached across the table and took her hands. Mma's chest squeezed tight. The older woman loved her like a daughter, evident in the way she smiled with kind eyes.

"You know my friend, Lami Abubakar?" She asked quietly

Mma nodded. "Aunty Lami? Yes, I do. You took me to her spa in Abuja once."

"And your mum almost killed me for that. Lami is in desperate need of an office manager to run her spa. She just opened one here in Ikoyi. If you are willing to work in a spa, I can give Lami a call. I am sure she will be delighted to offer you a job," Aunty Ekene went on to explain. "If you take the job, you can start on Monday."

She paused again and looked her niece squarely in the eye. "But it comes with a condition. Lami insists that her Spa Manager lives in the apartment within the Spa complex. Although, I do not think your mother would ever agree for you to take the job. You know she doesn't like my husband or his friends."

There was silence, then Mma shook her head. "I will take it."

"Mma…" Her aunt began, a warning note in her voice, but Mma held up her hands.

"My sisters are home from school because I have not been able to pay the school fees. I have used up the little money I make from cleaning in the hospital and the allowance you give me, which mummy stopped when she found out. We haven't eaten any meal for two days, just water and the landlord will ask for his rent in two weeks, so, yes, I will take this job."

"Mma, I have told you I will pay the rent," the older woman said again, shaking her head.

"And you have been doing that for two years!" Mma got up and went to kneel before her aunty. "I need this job, Aunty. In fact, the way I feel now, I will take any job I see. I will deal with mummy when I get home. I just turned twenty-four. I can't be sitting at home doing nothing." She looked up at her older relative, who was looking at her quietly. "Call Aunty Lami. I will take the job."

"Are you sure?" Aunty Ekene had a worried look on her face.

Mma understood why her Aunty was worried. If there was one thing Aunty Ekene and her husband didn't want, it was trouble with Mma's mother. When her mother was angry, she lost it, and she could curse like mad.

Mma shook her head slowly, remembering the troubles her aunt her gone through.

When her aunt married Lotanna, Ekene's father disowned her because she didn't wed the chief her father preferred. As if that wasn't bad enough, Mma's mother, Ginika, supported the old man and rained abuse on Ekene, thereby hurting her more.

They didn't attend Ekene's wedding. But Lotanna's parents had rallied around her and stood by her. Afterwards, Ekene tried to reach out, but her father and sister did not want anything to do with her. Despite this, she refused to turn her back on Mma and her siblings. Her love for her nieces was obvious. She continued to support them. First had been paying Mma's university tuition, and now it was the twins. They could always count on their aunt.

"Are you sure?" her aunt asked again.

Mma nodded, hugged the woman hard and stood. "Please call her while I finish cooking the soup I promised to cook for you."

Aunty Ekene shook her head. "I am going to call Lami. If your mother comes for me, I will strangle you!"

Mma laughed. "Mummy loves you. She's just angry and afraid of Grandpa and how he reacts when your name is mentioned. You know mummy lives for his approval."

"For how long? It's been over 10 years, and honestly, I really do not care anymore." Then, she asked, "How is your grandfather, by the way?"

She got up, following her niece to the kitchen.

"You mean your father?" Mma asked, a mischievous smile on her face. "He's fine. He is coming this weekend." She turned to look at her aunty, who was rummaging through her handbag for her mobile phone. "You miss him, don't you?"

"I can't kill myself, Mma." The woman found her phone and waved it at her niece. "I'm going to call Lami. Cook my oha soup. I am starving."

She walked back into the living room, already dialling her friend's number. A little while later, Aunty Ekene returned. "Nne, you got the job. Starting salary: ₦200,000, one-bed apartment within the complex and use of the spa company car."

"Oh my God! Aunty Ekene!" Screamed Mma. She flew across the kitchen and enveloped the woman in a hug, holding her tight as tears ran down her cheeks. "Aunty, God bless you!" she kept repeating as her Aunty patted her back.

"It's Okay. I just feel bad that it had to come to this before you could come to me for help." She waved her phone at her niece. "You need to figure out what to tell your mother because she is going to be livid. I do not want to be involved at all, especially as your grandfather will be around. I think you should tell her over the phone and give her time to get angry and calm down."

"Mummy...." Mma began explaining, but Aunty shook her head

"You have to deal with this immediately. You and I know she is going to be livid."

Mma nodded. "Let me cross that bridge when I get to it."

***

"Who was that?" Fuad Danjuma asked his sister Lami as she hung up her call. They were sitting in her office in her new spa in Ikoyi.

Lami met his gaze as she placed her phone on the table. She was a beautiful, soft-spoken woman in her forties.

"Ekene. She called about her niece, Mma. She's a lovely girl."

Fuad nodded. "How is Ekene? I haven't seen her in a while."

Lami and Ekene had been friends for over ten years. They'd met when Ekene married Lotanna. Their husbands were childhood friends, and the women had become remarkably close friends since then.

"She's fine. By the way, are you coming over to the house today?" his sister asked.

"Today is Friday, and you know I don't do family visits on Friday. Have you forgotten it's Ike's birthday?" Fuad fidgeted with his watch and redirected the conversation away from himself. "Was it Ekene's niece you were offering a job?"

"Yes. A very delightful young woman," his sister replied.

"Good for her," he said, getting to his feet. "I've got to run."

"Fuad," there was a warning note in his sister's voice, "Your mother is in my house. If you do not come by to greet her this evening, I will bring her to your house tomorrow morning, and you know what that means. You know your mother, ba? I don't need to refresh your memory at all, do I?"

"Aww, sis, you know why I am avoiding her," protested Fuad. "Haba, she keeps wanting to know when Aisha and I will start preparations for the wedding. I am not ready to get married yet," he added, winking at his sister, who simply shook her head in confusion.

"She's not wrong, you know! What are you both waiting for? It's a known fact that you both will eventually get married, so why wait? I am tired of Uwa calling me and asking me to speak to you! Are you not tired of a different girl every other weekend? You sleep with anything in a skirt that walks by you! I can't understand why you think it's okay to treat women the way you treat them. Love them and leave them, right? And you are supposed to be in a relationship!"

She got up, came around the desk and escorted him out of her office.

"I treat the ladies I date well, and contrary to what you think, I do not have a different girl every weekend. Yes, I am in a relationship with Aisha. But right now, I'm not sure about where it is heading. I know one thing, though, I am not ready to get married. When I am ready, you will be the first to know." He dropped a kiss on her forehead, a grin on his face. "So, be a good sister, go home, cook dinner for your husband and kids. I will see Uwa tomorrow morning, deal?"

He used the fond term they used for their mother as a diversionary tactic, but it didn't seem to work.

"Oh, shut up, Fuad! What exactly is the problem? Why are you delaying the inevitable? Aisha and her mother have been talking to Uwa and putting pressure on her by dropping subtle hints, and Uwa is tired! So, what exactly is the issue?" His sister scowled.

Fuad sighed. "I'm not sure I want to marry Aisha."

"Ha! Mene ne wannan?" Lami spoke in Hausa, her shock apparent. "Fuad, you are kidding, right? Walahi, you do not want to go there." She moved away from her brother, a frown marring her perfect face. "I tell you. You do not want to go there. Uwa will kill you."

"Listen, Lami, can we not talk about this now? This will sort itself out."

Fuad didn't like talking about his relationship with Aisha. They had been together for almost two years now. Their mothers had pushed them into a relationship. Fuad should have resisted both mothers. But to please his parent, who had still been getting herself back after his father's death, he had gone along with her plans hoping it would ease the pain of her grief. Big Mistake. Lami had warned him then. She had never been a fan of Aisha.

"I wish you had taken my advice not to get involved with Aisha," she mumbled as though she read his mind as she went back and settled in her chair. "Go ahead, I will handle Uwa, but be at the house tomorrow to see her before she leaves for her Dubai trip."

"You know I will. Love you, sis." Fuad grinned as he swept out of the office.

He had more jubilant plans, like his friend's birthday celebrations which he had been looking forward to all week. So, he shoved Uwa, Aisha, her mother, and their wedding machinations aside. No way in hell was he going to allow thoughts of marriage to spoil his mood.

He wasn't ready to settle down yet. Not when he had an idea of the kind of woman he wanted to spend the rest of his life with. He was determined that when he wedded, it would be to a kind-hearted and decent woman of his own choosing.

Not Aisha.

Initially, when he met Aisha, he had been optimistic about the relationship, although it was an arranged one. However, a couple of weeks later, he changed his tune.

Aisha was not the woman for him.

Granted, she was beautiful, but her character was nothing to write home about. She was a condescending person. Their last outing together, where she had slapped a waiter for spilling drinks on her, was still very fresh in Fuad's mind.

Recently, he started making excuses each time she wanted to see him. All he could think about was how he would end the relationship without causing his mum distress as she desperately wanted him to settle down. The campaign to get him married commenced months ago when he turned thirty-four.

And gained momentum when he'd started dating Aisha.

Thinking of Aisha, he frowned as he recalled the last time she had visited him at work. She had barged into his office, spoiling for a fight as usual. Her issue—his philandering ways were causing her embarrassment.

She was also livid because he had been making excuses not to see her.

Fuad had simply shrugged. He's told her to call it quits with him if she didn't trust him or to stop listening to rumours about him cheating on her and learn to trust him if their relationship would work.

His comment had earned him a slap, and she had stormed out of his office in tears.

Dismayed, Fuad had followed her immediately apologetic. Still, Aisha had been livid, screaming at him to get out of her life and then she had called his mother and sobbed out her heart to her.

Fuad hated it when she did that, especially as he had spent almost an hour on the phone listening to his mother rant at him about Aisha.

In the Northern part of Nigeria, where he came from, arranged marriages, especially amongst the elites was customary. So, initially, he hadn't been averse to the idea of marrying Aisha. However, now he wasn't so sure.

His greatest fear was marrying a callous woman. Sadly, he was beginning to see that Aisha was that kind of woman,

Walking into the parking lot, he smiled at his sister's driver, who handed over his car keys. Thanking him, Fuad got into his car and drove towards Lekki Phase One, where he was meeting Ike and Mahmud.

No, he wasn't ready to get married. When the time was right, when he met the right woman, he would know.

CHAPTER TWO

"Over my dead body!" Mrs Nwachukwu screamed at the top of her voice. "Papa, did you hear what this ingrate, this ungrateful granddaughter of yours said?"

Mma sat on the sofa with her sisters, holding hands and watching their mother pace round the small and cramped living room. She shouldn't have come home. Maybe she should have taken Aunty Ekene's advice and told her mother over the phone about her new job.

It was almost two o'clock. Mma was supposed to meet Aunty Lami at the spa in Ikoyi by 4pm to collect the keys to her new apartment. Yet she was at home, afraid of how her mother would react to news of her new job.

"Do you have an alternative solution, Mummy?" Kelechi, her younger sister, asked. "I mean, we have been home for two weeks now because we haven't paid our school fees. We can hardly feed. Moreover, our rent is due next week. So, I ask you again, Mummy, do you have a solution? If you do, then Mma can forfeit the job. If you don't, Mma will take the job. She needs it."

Her mother whirled around just as their grandfather, who'd just finished his lunch, surged to his feet. His face scrunched in anger as he stalked to his granddaughters sitting together on the sofa, looking nervously at their mother.

"You will not speak to your mother like that. And Mma?" He turned to her. "You will turn down that job. Ekene is dead to this family. I do not understand why you are still in touch with her. I have banned you from contacting her, but it seems like all my warnings have fallen on deaf ears. You and your sisters have kept in touch with your Aunty and her husband, and I will not have it."

Mma saw red.

They weren't offering any solutions, just issuing orders which didn't help their current situation. She would not back down, not this time. Shaking her head, she slowly got to her feet to stand before her grandfather. She was going to get into trouble, but she was past caring.

They couldn't go on like this any longer, and if Aunty was offering her a job, she would take it.

"Why Papa?" she asked quietly, watching him.

"Because I say so!" he thundered.

"Papa, I'm sorry. I am taking the job. We need it to survive," she replied immediately, shaking her head in disbelief.

She wasn't ready for the slap that followed. Her head snapped back, and she tasted blood. Her eyes filling with tears, she stepped back and forcefully repeated, "I am taking the job unless you and Mama have another option for me."

"Then you are not welcome in this house! Leave at once!" Her mother screamed, pointing towards the front door.

Mma and her sisters, Kelechi and Kaira, had anticipated that this would be the outcome of her decision to work with Lami Abubakar. She wasn't surprised at her mother's reaction, but she also wasn't going to back down. She had her life and her sisters to think of. If working with Lami Abubakar would guarantee them a better life, she would accept the job.

Aunty Ekene had already given the girls sufficient money to pay their school fees, and they would leave for school in two days.

Mma watched as her mother turned away from her, her anger evident on her face.

Shaking her head slowly, the tears running down her cheeks, she turned to leave the sitting room. She was tired, and to be honest, she was looking forward to moving out. The fights, abuse, and constant bickering were getting to her and taking a toll on the sisters.

They could speak to their mother, and she would understand. But their grandfather would always have a hold over her and control her actions. Mma was used to her mother constantly fighting Aunty Ekene simply because it pleased their grandfather, and she didn't want to be in his bad books.

But Mma was headstrong, like her father. The twins were easier for their mother to control when Mma wasn't around. Still, the siblings rallied around when Mma was home and stood up for each other, no matter the situation.

The problem was, Papa had disowned their aunt, and his word was law.

Unlike Aunty Ekene, Ginika had always been weak and scared of the old man. Growing up, Ekene had stood up to her father and refused to allow him to bully her. In contrast, Ginika had been the scared daughter, always doing what her parents wanted.

Now, Mma was exhibiting the same traits as Ekene. Mma was the granddaughter that stood up to her grandfather and refused to be cowed by him. Mma could never understand how a father would encourage his children to fight and not speak to each other.

Kaira and Kelechi got up to follow their sister, giving their grandfather a dirty look as they left the living room and went to help Mma pack.

***

An hour later, all three sisters arrived at Aunty Ekene's waterfront mansion in Ikoyi, but she had already left for work. Their aunt had left instructions with the driver to take Mma to Lami Abubakar's office, where Lami was waiting for Mma.

"You are sure you will be fine?" Kaira asked. She was the quiet one, very level-headed, always wanting to make peace.

"Of course, I will. Aunty said you can go with me to the Spa."

Her sisters shook their heads.

"No, Mma, even though you are only going to get the keys to your new apartment, it won't be professional if we all turn up at your new place of work. Meet Aunty Lami, get the keys to your new place and then give us a call. We will come over later this evening to see you." This time, it was Kelechi who spoke.

Mma looked at her younger sisters, her eyes filling with tears. Kaira was the first to hug her, followed by Kelechi. She was going to miss them. The sisters shared a solid bond and had always stuck together through thick or thin.

She was going to miss their late-night talks, their movie nights and their time spent cooking together, but taking this job was for the best. She owed it to them, to her mother and to herself to become something in life.

***

Lami was waiting by the reception when Ekene's car drove into the spa parking lot. A smile lit up her face when Mma emerged from the vehicle and began walking towards the building.

Immediately Mma walked through the revolving glass doors, she sighted Lami standing by the reception desk, which on its own was a work of art.

Every time Mma saw her aunt's friend, she couldn't help staring.

Lami Abubakar was simply breath-taking. She was what Nigerians popularly referred to as a stunning beauty. She was a tall woman with chocolate coloured skin. With her pointed nose, and almond-shaped brown eyes, which was synonymous with women of the Fulani tribe, Lami turned heads wherever she went.

Mma smiled as Lami stepped forward and enveloped her in a hug.

"Aunty Lami, good afternoon."

"Mma, how are you, dear?" Lami smiled, stepping back to look her up and down. "You look amazing."

"I'm fine, Aunty Lami. Thank you so much for offering me a job."

"Aww, I am the one who should be glad you took the job. You don't know how relieved I am that I have someone I can trust in charge. Come on, dear, let me show you around." Lami smiled at Mma, who fell into step behind her. "This is my first spa-slash-health club in Lagos. You know I already have one in Abuja, right?"

Mma nodded in reply. "I have been there once. Aunty Ekene took me to visit. You were out of the country."

Mma would never forget that visit. Her mother had almost lynched Aunty Ekene for taking her to Abuja. As usual, her grandfather had gotten involved and had blown it out of proportion.

"This is much bigger, though. It has a pool, a gym, a restaurant and a health store," Lami explained as they walked through the building. "The restaurant is already a hit. Our club sandwich is something you must try. We've already been featured in 'Lost in Lagos'!"

"I know. I read the edition that featured you. The décor is unique. The pictures they took don't do this place justice," Mma replied as she followed Lami through an open door and into an office.

"Your office." Lami opened the blinds.

"Wow" was all Mma said as she came to a stop and looked around the place. She loved the decoration, elegant and straightforward and her office was big. No, it was massive! One side was glass, and it overlooked the pool. It had a lovely relaxing view.

"This is really nice, Aunty Lami" Lami could tell she was excited as she turned to face her. "The décor is amazing, much nicer than the one in Abuja."

"Ah! Don't say this in front of my brother. He set this up and oversaw the interior décor from beginning to end. He's had his head in the clouds since it opened and got featured in Lost in Lagos! His bragging is driving me nuts!"

"Well, he should! This place is awesome."

Lami laughed. "Let me show you to your apartment."

A hedge demarcated her apartment from the pool, and it was more than she had bargained for. A one-bed apartment, fully furnished and equipped with all the latest gadgets, including a land phone connecting to the gatehouse and the spa.

Mma was stunned as she surveyed the well-furnished apartment. It was beautiful and comfy, and it was all hers. She couldn't believe that she would be living here, and she would also have a company car and driver at her disposal.

This was too good to be true!

"You like it? Would you like to change anything in here?" asked Lami.

"Change, Aunty Lami? Kai, this is heaven! You and Aunty Ekene are amazing. I'm blessed to have you both in my life," she said, her eyes filling with tears as she walked over to the older woman and hugged her. "God bless you both, thank you. I won't let you both down."

"I know, Mma, which is why you are here. I'll leave you to settle in as I must head out now. Since today is Friday, use this weekend to settle in, and you resume on Monday, okay?"

Mma nodded, taking a step back. "I will. Thank you once again, Aunty Lami."

"No problem, my dear," Lami replied. She gave Mma one last smile and then turned and left the apartment.

Immediately, Mma reached for her phone and dialled Kelechi's number.

Her sister picked up after the first ring.

"How far? Where are you guys?" she asked.

"We are still in Aunty Ekene's house. What's up, any gist? How did it go with Aunty Lami?"

"You should see my apartment! Oh my God! I am so excited!"

"Wonderful," Kelechi said. "I'm giving Kaira a thumbs-up sign."

"Please find your way here, oh!" Mma said, her voice grew bubbly as she continued, "We have to celebrate this night! We must wash this job and my new house oh! Name the place, and we are good to go, oh."

"You? Go where? Biko, Kaira and I have an outing. We are meeting friends at Quilox. Next thing now, you will take us to KFC for the outing!" Kelechi replied, followed by a burst of laughter through the phone from Kaira.

Mma crinkled her nose and shook her head. Her sisters always referred to her as a prude, granted she wasn't as hip as them. Still, she wasn't that bad either, and tonight she was determined to go out and celebrate her job and new apartment. Tonight was the night, a new, bolder, and more confident Mma emerged. So, they wanted to go to Quilox? She would go too and dance the night away. She deserved it.

"Pick me up on your way to Quilox." She struggled to hold her laughter as she heard her sisters gasp over the phone. She could just picture Kelechi with her mouth wide open in shock.

Kaira took the phone from Kelechi and spoke into the mouthpiece. "Hmm, Mma, are you sure?"

"Ehen now, I am getting ready now."

"Okay, oh. Please don't wear a bubu. We will be there in thirty minutes," Kaira said. "Wear something hip, biko. We have a reputation to maintain. Our older sister cannot be looking like our Aunty when we go out."

"Shut up and get here soon." Mma hung up the phone on her sister's laughter, muttering under her breath.

Her sisters were right to laugh. She had never really gone out that much.

During her four years in the university, she alternated between lectures, church, mid-week fellowships, and bible study groups. Her sisters were outgoing. Even Lola, her childhood friend who was due in Nigeria next week, had a highly active social life.

The only date she had ever been on was in her first year at the university. And after she had freaked out when her date kissed her, he had never contacted her again. She was sure he had told people she was a prude because nobody else asked her out again throughout her time at the university.

Not that it bothered her, she had been glad because it had given her time to focus on her studies. But all that was about to change. She was determined to go out today and enjoy before she began work on Monday. She owed herself a little bit of fun.

Sighing, she walked into the living room and opened the suitcase of new clothes Aunty Ekene had gifted her with.

New clothes, new life, new job.

Thirty minutes later, she was ready. She had settled for jeans, a silk top that she could tuck in, and a pair of high sandals. Mma was tall, and in those sandals, she was almost 6'1.

Her hair, which she considered her best feature, was up in a bun. Admiring herself in the mirror, she smiled.

Her crazy sisters could not fault her dressing at all.

Tonight, she was launching the new Mma Nwachukwu, Confident and beautiful.

CHAPTER THREE

Club Quilox was busy as usual. Since the club opened, it'd become one of the hottest venues on the Lagos scene and the place to be on a Friday night.

Fuad loved hanging out here. It was trendy, had a relaxed atmosphere with great food and drinks and a fantastic DJ.

Tonight, he and his friends were celebrating Ike's birthday. They had all decided not to come with their partners. Good thing because Fuad was currently avoiding Aisha after she slapped him in his office.

Tonight, he was determined to have fun, then he would visit his mother tomorrow and then pay Aisha a visit. He hoped she would be in a much better mood by then.

He was sitting by the bar, drink in hand when three beautiful ladies walked into the club. He sat up immediately and blinked.

His friend, Ike and his cousin, Mahmud, each holding a glass of scotch, also sat up whistling in appreciation. They, too, had noticed the latest arrivals.

Who wouldn't? They were stunning women, especially the taller one wearing tight-fitting jeans.

"Why are you whistling?" Fuad asked, raising an eyebrow at Ike and Mahmud, who stared past him to where the three ladies had stopped by a group of people and were exchanging hugs and greetings.

"Wow," was all Ike said, taking a swig from a glass of scotch in his hand. "Hot-looking ladies."

"You can say that again," Mahmud said from behind him.

Fuad shook his head, the corner of his eyes crinkling, as he watched the women. He smiled then turned back to point his bottle at his friends.

"You both are engaged, marriage dates set, so I ask again why you are whistling?"

"Oh, shut up, Fuad," Ike hissed, turning to beckon a waiter over as Fuad burst into laughter.

"Not my fault. You are too scared to either call it quits with Aisha or to marry her," said Ike, eyeing him.

"Don't mind the coward. I can't believe how scared you are of calling it quits with Aisha. Because you are afraid of the fallout if you do break up with her," Mahmud chirped in from behind, giving Fuad a withering look.

Fuad simply laughed and turned to look towards the group.

Leaning back, he continued to watch the group of friends as they chatted excitedly. His focus, though, was on the tallest lady in their midst.

Fuad had seen beautiful women in his life, but she was by far the most exquisite he had seen. She wore heels, but he could see that she was tall. Instantly he made a decision. He had to meet her.

Tossing back his drink, he placed his bottle on the bar and straightened up.

"Where are you going?" Mahmud asked, eyeing him.

Fuad shrugged, raising an eyebrow. "To introduce myself to that beautiful lady that just walked in." Then, he added slyly, "Not my fault, you and Ike are already taken, and you can only look but not touch. I, on the other hand, can look and touch. Excuse me."

He walked away, chuckling, ignoring the deadly stares Ike and Mahmud were giving him.

"It's supposed to be a guys-only night," Ike threw at him in disgust.

"I hear you," Fuad tossed his reply over his shoulder, grinning as he made his way across the floor towards the ladies.

***

Kelechi turned and whispered to Kaira, and Mma overheard. "One fine brother is coming towards us."

"Which one?" Kaira and Mma turned and saw the man walking towards them.

"Whew, kai, he is fine, oh," Kelechi whispered back as she and her twin turned to watch the man striding towards them.

"Hi," he said to Kelechi and Kaira, who smiled back at him.

"Hi," the twins chorused in unison, smiling at the stranger.

He nodded at them, then moved towards Mma, who was standing to one side. She had ignored his approach and scrolled through her phone. The man nodded towards Mma, indicating that he wanted to speak to her and mouthed 'thanks' as Kelechi and Kaira smiled and moved away.

Mma looked up as he came to stand before her and almost lost her breath as her heart slammed into her chest.

Up close, he was stunning. Sliding his hands into his pockets, he inclined his head and grinned at her.

"Hey," he said

She smiled shyly. "Hi."

"I'm Fuad." He extended a hand, and she took it hesitantly.

She wasn't used to attracting attention like this. Certainly not enough for a man to chat her up. "My name is Mma."

"Hey, Mma, my friends and I are by the bar. Would you like to join us for a while? We don't bite," he said as his eyes lit up in amusement.

Her face furrowed, and she glanced at her sisters.

Kelechi gave a thumbs-up sign from behind Fuad. She winked at Kaira, who nodded at Mma and then turned back to her group of friends.

"I will kill them," Mma muttered under her breath. The twins had effectively abandoned her with this stranger.

Fuad was still waiting for an answer.

"Hey, trust me, we don't bite. My friends and I are actually great fun, you know," he said, a teasing smile on his face.

He turned to nod towards her sisters. "If it makes you feel better, your friends can join too."

She glanced past him to where the two men sitting by the bar. They smiled at her and gave her a thumbs-up sign, making comical faces at Fuad.

Mma laughed, turning to Fuad. "Your friends seem nice. Fine, lead the way. I am sure my sisters would love to join too."

"Atta girl," Fuad grinned, taking her arm to lead her to his friends, who were watching their approach with apparent interest.

***

He introduced her to his two friends, Ike and Mahmud, while he pulled a stool to the bar.

"Thank you," she said as she sat on it.

Fuad turned to smile at her. "What would you like to drink?"

"A margarita is fine," she replied. She had never taken alcohol before. Still, she wouldn't act like a prude and ask for a coke or glass of juice in front of Fuad and his friends.

She watched as he summoned the waiter and placed her order, then he turned to her with a lazy smile.

"Thanks for joining us and saving me from these two boring friends of mine." He grinned, exposing perfect white teeth, doubling up in laughter as Ike gave him a stiff jab in the ribs.

"Really, Mahmud and I were tolerating your boring presence! We should be thanking her," Ike retorted, rolling his eyes at Fuad.

Three glasses later, Mma was feeling lightheaded. She should not have had more than a glass, but it was easy to just keep ordering drinks. She was having so much fun. Fuad and his friends were easy to talk to and fun to be with. They had moved to the VIP room when her sisters, and their friends, had come over to join them.

She was conscious of the fact that Fuad kept glancing at her most of the time, and to her annoyance, her sisters noticed it too and couldn't stop smirking and eyeballing her. Ignoring them, she turned to face Ike, who was speaking to Fuad. She would deal with her sisters much later when they got home. Mma hadn't had this much fun in years. But truth be told, she had to admit she was flattered by the attention Fuad gave her.

Damn, but he was fine. Mma snuck a glance at him from beneath her lowered lashes. Almost every woman in the room was sneaking looks at him. He oozed charm and charisma, and he had the aura of someone who had money too.

Suddenly, she found herself wishing that it was just the two of them alone. What would it be like to kiss him? To be kissed by someone that looked like him would be a dream come true. Then she shook her head in mortification, embarrassed at the direction of her thoughts. Of course, it was just the alcohol talking. She couldn't be lusting after someone she barely knew.

After a while, she started feeling tired and glancing at her watch. She smiled apologetically at Fuad, who raised an eyebrow at her as she leaned toward her sisters.

"Are we leaving anytime soon?" She wanted to know because her sisters looked like the party was just getting started.

Kelechi nodded. "Yes, we are. But we are heading someplace else. We are crashing at yours today, so we can all go together."

"Not for me, Kele. I must head home. I'm tired. Don't worry about me, though. Will call an Uber. You guys go ahead and have fun."

"But..." Kelechi began, a worried look on her face.

"Don't worry, Kele. I am fine. Please go and have fun. Biko." Mma was already scrolling through her phone for an Uber number.

Fuad stopped her by covering her hand with his. Mma's skin tingled where he touched her, and she turned to look at him in confusion, her cheeks hot.

"I am actually about to leave. I can drop you off if you like. I am staying in Ikoyi, Banana Island. Where do you stay?" he asked, ignoring Mahmud, who stood and stared at him with a quirked brow.

"Ikoyi, I stay in Ikoyi too," Mma replied, smiling at him. "Thank you. if it's no bother and won't take you out of your way."

"No bother at all. It will be my pleasure. I'm ready when you are." He flashed a smile.

Mma was sure that if she wasn't sitting down, her knees would have given away.

He had an amazing smile, and right now, all she could think of was kissing him. Then, mentally slapping herself, she turned to speak to her sisters, who were looking excited at the fact that she had accepted a ride home with a stranger.

"What are you doing?" Mahmud leaned over to whisper to Fuad.

Mma pretended she couldn't hear the men talking.

"Taking a lady home, Mahmud."

"Home? Fuad, we have a party to head to. Invite her along. You know, you can't bail out now," Mahmud insisted, as Fuad got up to his feet

"Ike, say something," Mahmud muttered, turning towards Ike, who was leaning in his seat watching Fuad. Ike glanced at Mma, then he turned back to Mahmud and raised an eyebrow.

"Something must be wrong with you, Mahmud. Now, if you are done giving Fuad a lecture, let me know, so we can start heading out to Bella's party. I don't have the energy to explain why I am late to Bella."

He too got to his feet to give Fuad a hug, "See you later, Bro. Talk tomorrow."

Fuad nodded, reaching out to thump a glowering Mahmud on the shoulder as Mma came to stand beside him.

"Ready?" He looked down at her.

She nodded with a smile.

'Let's go then. I will need your address."

***

The car park was busy as usual, with people standing around in groups, holding drinks and chatting.

As a VIP customer, Fuad could park on a reserved spot. He nodded casually at the valet, who directed him to his vehicle.

He drove the latest model, black Range Rover Autobiography.

Was he really going to take her home as promised? Fuad asked himself as they got into his car, and he drove out of the club premises.

Did he really want to? When all he wanted to do was kiss her senseless. Hell, that was all he had been thinking about the entire time they were together in the club.

He hadn't been able to take his eyes off her all night.

Granted, many people considered him to be a player. But he never cheated when he was in a relationship. And he was in one now.

Still, being near Mma and not touching her was driving him nuts.

He loved women, loved everything about them, and he also loved sex. Who didn't? And right now, all he could think of was getting Mma into his bed.

He didn't pick up unknown women, and he didn't do one-night stands. But something about Mma was pushing him to break the rules. And right now, all he wanted to do was bed her.

He turned to her, intending to ask for her address. The sooner he dropped her off, the better for him. Then he would go home and have a cold shower.

"Would you like to still hang out?" he said instead. "We could get Glover Court suya and have a nightcap at mine. I promise to drop you off at home by midnight, and you will love Glover Court suya."

Once the words expunged from him, he groaned inwardly. What was he thinking?

"That would be great."

Her response surprised him. Perhaps she wasn't ready for the evening to end too. The night was still young.

Fuad smiled, put his car into gear and reversed out of the car park. He drove to Glover Road, Ikoyi, where they got suya, and then Fuad went to his house in Banana Island. His home was on a quiet leafy street in the estate. He drove into the compound and parked near three other covered vehicles, and then he turned and smiled at her.

***

The inside of Fuad's house was spectacular and tastefully done. He used lots of wood and house plants to a wonderful effect.

"This is beautiful, Fuad," Mma said in awe, turning around. "Very artistic. You've used a lot of wood too."

"You think?" Fuad watched her walk around, a look of amazement on her face as she took in the décor.

He could hear his heart beating hard. Why had he brought her here? What was he thinking? They were strangers, and he had never brought a stranger to his house. The only person who had ever been here was Aisha, and she had never stayed over.

No overnight stay until after marriage. That was his rule, and Aisha was okay with it. So why had he brought Mma here? Deep inside, he wanted her to stay the night. He didn't know how to convince her to stay, but he would try.

"Yes, it's unique. You have an amazing taste." She replied quietly, turning towards him.

He shoved his hands in his pockets to stop from reaching for her. Tension arced in the air. He needed to diffuse it before they both did something they would regret. This was a first for him.

"The suya?" she asked, raising an eyebrow.

He smiled and nodded, a sigh of relief escaping.

"Take a seat, and I will get something for us to drink. What would you like?" He threw over his shoulder as he strode in the direction of the kitchen.

"A soft drink, please. I think I've had enough alcohol for today," her amused voice reached him, and he chuckled.

An hour later, they had consumed the entire suya and were laughing hilariously at jokes from their pasts.

"You are fun to be with," Fuad said after a while, leaning back in his seat to watch her. "And very easy to talk to."

"You too," was her instant reply. "I have never had this much fun, and this suya is so tasty."

"Really? Don't worry, I know a couple of hidden suya joints I discovered. Stick with me, and I will take you there one of these days. Come on, let me have your address. I have to get you home, I promised to drop you off, and it's almost midnight," he said, glancing at his wristwatch.

He got to his feet, holding out a hand to pull her up. She placed her hand in his and got to her feet. That's when everything changed.

Fuad was looking down at her hands, playing with her fingers.

"Stay a little bit longer," he said softly.

His heart began pounding. He was sure she could hear it. She tried to pull her hand away, but he held on to it, tugging her toward him till their foreheads were touching.

"Stay. We will just talk, get to know more about each other," he whispered, looking into her eyes. He was desperate to hold her in his arms and kiss her, but he was worried she would think he was coming on too strong.

Mma's throat rippled as she swallowed hard. She tried to move away, but his other arm went around her waist to hold her.

"I can't, Fuad. I shouldn't have come here. You should have taken me home."

"Why?"

"I don't know. I'm probably scared of what might happen if I stay."

"So, what's the worst that could happen? I kiss you, you kiss me back," he replied quietly, watching her intently. "Would that be so bad? I'm not a bad kisser."

He tried to joke, but the expression on her face made his pulse pound.

Oh Lord, he would not be able to walk away from her. Not now. His heart was beating so fast. He stared at her, waiting for her reply. Would kissing him be so bad? Fuad wondered, would it be so bad to let himself go for once and indulge in a one-night stand?

Mma was gorgeous, and he was interested in her for the wrong reasons. But, one kiss wouldn't hurt, he told himself as he watched her struggle to decide.

She had a very expressive face, and he could guess her thoughts from just watching her.

She looked up at him. Then his heart slammed into his ribs as she stood on tiptoe, cupping his face. She leaned up and kissed him on the lips softly.

That was all the encouragement he needed. He pulled her closer and did what he had been aching to do all night. He kissed her slowly at first, pulling her in closer. Mma moaned, and pleasure washed over him. His hands were splayed across her back as his lips explored hers. His other hands held her chin in place as he broke the kiss and placed soft open-mouthed kisses along her neck curve.

He felt her shudder as she gripped his shoulders hard, her head tilted to expose her neck to his lips. He kissed the nape of her neck again, and she moaned, sliding her arms around his neck.

She was trembling now, he noticed. Good, she wasn't immune to his charms.

"You taste so good," he whispered, his hands tightening on her waist. "You smell and feel so nice."

He slid his palm under her silk shirt to feel her skin.

"Don't stop," she moaned as his lips returned to hers, kissing her softly.

"I don't intend to," he replied, backing her slowly towards the sofa.

She gasped when the back of her knees hit the sofa. She fell onto the cushions, and Fuad came down beside her.

For a moment, he was propped on his elbow, looking down at her, his heart beating so fast, he was sure it would burst. Then he leaned over and claimed her lips in a kiss, his hands sliding further to trace her ribcage and curve around her back, holding her in place as he kissed her.

It was supposed to be one kiss, just one kiss, but he went up in flames and gave a groan of satisfaction as her hands crept under his polo top to trace the muscles on his back. At her touch, Fuad lit up like fire, and he shifted until he covered her with his body.

He tensed when she reached for his polo top and proceeded to tug it off. Pulling away, he scrutinised her face. "Are you comfortable with this?"

When she nodded, he sat up. Yanking the top over his head, he tossed it on the floor and continued kissing her.

"Oh, please. Don't. stop." Mma gasped when he suddenly moved off her.

"I'm not stopping, babe," he whispered as he reached down to pull her silk top over her head, then he tasted her again.

She felt so good, he thought. Kissing her felt so good.

"Are you sure, Mma?" He asked in between caresses, his hands pausing over the clasp of her jeans.

"Yes," she whispered against his lips. "Oh, yes."

***

She was gone by the time he woke up.

Fuad was livid. He had never had a girl run out on him after a night together. Scratch that he had never had a girl spend the night in his house.

He drew the line at that. As far as he was concerned, only his wife deserved the honour of spending the night in his bed, in his house.

Yet he had brought a stranger home, a first for him. He groaned when he recalled how he had spent a better part of the night making love to her. The best sex he'd had in his life.

And she had taken off before he woke up!

She had also been a virgin.

He swore angrily, striding out of his room to confront his staff, who had let her leave without informing him. How on earth had she managed to leave that early, and why hadn't they told him? A couple of minutes later, he found out that she had called for a cab and had asked his staff not to wake him up, that she would call him later. Which was a lie because she didn't have his number. Neither did he have hers, nor had he managed to get her address.

Fuad felt like a fool. Striding back into his room, he snatched the note she had left on the dresser. This was another first for him. She had left nothing, not her phone number or an address, just a note saying.

"Thank you for an amazing night."

"Thank you for an amazing night? Hell!" he swore under his breath.

In anger, he flung the note across the room, cursing under his breath as he went to take a shower. How could she go just like that, leaving a message saying thank you? If she didn't want to see him again, she could have waited to at least say goodbye properly.

They had connected on a deep level. He had never interacted with any woman like that. Never met any woman he could converse with so easily and laugh with so readily. So how had he not gotten her number before they left the club?

He was so angry and felt foolish.

For the first time in his life, Fuad Danjuma was at a loss on what to do.

CHAPTER FOUR

Mma spent the better part of the weekend in her new apartment, getting ready for her new job and thinking about Fuad. She'd had a fantastic night. It was the best night of her life, not that she had any other experience to compare it to. But it had been a wonderful experience.

But that was all it was—an amazing night with a stranger, which was why, when she woke up, she had panicked and run out of the apartment. One kiss had led to another kiss and another kiss and another, and they had ended up in Fuad's bed where they had spent the better part of the night making love.

She, who'd never been on a date, had jumped into bed with the first man who'd shown an interest. She'd thrown caution to the winds.

He had made love to her all night long, and to her embarrassment, she hadn't wanted him to stop.

At least they had been smart enough to use protection. She remembered the look of shock on his face when he'd discovered she had been a virgin. When he had tried to ask her why she had grabbed his head and kissed him, and Fuad had forgotten his question.

Her sisters had arrived this morning eager to hear about Fuad, but she told them nothing happened. Now, she dreaded going out there to face her siblings.

Summoning up courage, she strode out of her room and into the kitchen where Kelechi was dishing out lunch.

For a one-bedroom apartment, the kitchen was huge, with an island that served as a mini breakfast table. Mma settled onto one of the stools and accepted a plate of steaming jollof rice minus meat that Kelechi passed to her.

Surprised, she turned to look at Kaira's plate. It had two pieces of fried chicken and fried plantain.

"What is this?" Mma gestured towards her plate of jollof rice.

"Food," Kelechi replied, settling down with her own plate of jollof rice, plus two pieces of fried chicken and plantain.

"Food? Where's my meat and plantain?"

"No meat!" her sisters from hell replied in unison. Kaira heaped a spoon of rice into her mouth. "Till you tell Kelechi and me what happened Friday night. Please don't lie. We came back here Friday after midnight. You hadn't returned, so we had to stay at Angela's house."

"So, spill," Kelechi chirped in gleefully.

So, they wanted to hear it all? She would gladly tell them. What was there to hide anyway?

She smiled, turned to face her sisters, took a deep breath, and spoke. "I slept with him. I had the most amazing night, making love to the most gorgeous man I have ever set my eyes on. There you have it. Is there anything else you would like to know?"

She grinned in satisfaction as her meddling sisters choked on their food, coughing hard as they both reached for the water.

Serves them right, nosy busybodies, Mma thought as she watched them sputter and tried to regain control after gulping down water.

"You what?" Kaira asked after managing to calm down. "You are kidding, right? Kelechi, did you hear her?"

"I did," Kelechi replied.

Mma almost laughed aloud as they abandoned their food and pulled up their stools closer to their sister.

"Repeat what you just said, Mma," Kelechi said.

"Are you both deaf?" Mma asked again as her lips turned up in a smile. She was trying hard not to laugh at the expressions on their faces.

They looked stunned, their mouths hanging open in shock.

"Nwanne, you are lying, right?" This was from Kaira, the ever sensible and calm sister.

"Nope. I wish I could show you proof, but I can't. I had mind-blowing sex. It was the ultimate one-night stand. I had amazing sex with Fuad, and I don't regret it one bit. What else would you like to know about my night with Fuad?" Mma said calmly, folding her arms.

She was staring at her sisters, who looked at her in shock. They both shook their head in unison while Kelechi passed her a plate of fried chicken.

"Thank you, ladies," Mma smiled, helping herself to a couple of pieces of chicken. "Now, let's eat. I am famished."

***

"Can you please stop being a pain in the ass and just get off my case," Fuad hissed at Ike as he manoeuvred into the parking lot of the oasis and parked his car in the space reserved for him. "I should have just let you come on your own, and I shouldn't have told you about Mma."

"You mean she walked out on you? Wow, the player got played," Ike commented as Fuad got out of his car and slammed the door. "I'll be damned. I love her already."

"Just shut up already, will you?"

"Wow, that's a first for you, Fuad. The lady did a number on you. It's over two weeks since the episode, and you are still so bitter about it," Ike chirped, the corner of his mouth lifting.

He grinned and practically ran to keep up with Fuad, who was muttering curses under his breath as he strode towards the spa.

"Get lost, Ike!" Fuad said.

"At all! Fuad, I'm sticking to you like glue," Ike replied gleefully.

Fuad hissed as they strode towards the building that doubled as a health club/restaurant in his sister's spa complex. He, Ike, and Mahmud were meant to be having lunch here. Instead, Mahmud had just texted him to say Aisha had just shown up to the restaurant.

Fuad was not in a good mood. Definitely not in the mood for Aisha and her manipulative plans.

It was bad enough that he was still seething from his experience with Mma. He certainly didn't need Aisha harassing him about a marriage date.

She hadn't apologised for slapping him but had simply gone ahead to put plans in place for an engagement without his input. To make matters worse, his mother had helped her do it.

This weekend, he was going to fly to Minna to discuss Aisha with his mother. It was time he made his decision regarding their relationship.

Ike was right, though. Two weeks plus, he was still seething about Mma walking out on him.

He hadn't been able to get her out of his head. Her smile, her laugh, the way she felt when he kissed her. He couldn't stop thinking about her, and it was driving him nuts.

Was Mma even her real name?

Well, unless by some miracle he ran into her, he would never know.

He pushed open the revolving doors leading into the reception that served as a waiting room for the spa and the health store and came to a stop, causing Ike to bump into him.

"Fuad, hey easy man," Ike hissed, pushing at his shoulder.

But Fuad wasn't listening.

Standing next to his sister and Aisha, nodding at something Lami was saying, was Mma, looking stunning in a very chic and sporty outfit.

***

"What is she doing here?" Lami muttered under her breath as Mma came to stand beside her.

"Who?" asked Mma as she turned to look at the object of her boss's displeasure.

Walking towards them was a pretty, well-dressed lady.

The woman smiled as soon as she sighted Lami, but something about her smile made Mma uncomfortable.

She was about to ask Lami about the woman when her boss straightened up with a smile plastered on her face. "Aisha."

"Lami, how are you? This place is amazing!" The lady stopped beside them. The two women hugged each other.

Mma marvelled at how they both pretended and hid their dislike of each other.

She could tell from their body language that they were not comfortable with each other. Amazed at how they could disguise their true feelings, Mma wished she could do the same. She had a lot to learn from people that moved in this circle.

"And who is this?" The lady finally turned to her. She was no longer smiling as she looked Mma up and down.

"This is Mma, my manager," Lami said. "Mma, this is Aisha."

"Her soon to be sister-in-law," Aisha chirped in happily, putting her stamp on Lami's brother.

She had to be speaking about Lami's younger brother, who was responsible for the stunning interior décor of the spa.

Mma was yet to meet him. Mr Danjuma was the ultimate golden boy amongst the staff.

The spa employees worshipped the ground he walked upon, especially the females. They couldn't stop talking about how handsome he was and how they would love to be the woman in his life. He was regarded as a prince charming, attractive, and wealthy.

In fact, his nickname around the clubhouse was 'Eye-candy.'

Mma smiled at Aisha. "Pleased to meet you, Ms Aisha. Welcome to the spa. Are you here for lunch or to use the facilities?" she asked.

Aisha sized her up, then dismissed her with a toss of her hair.

Mma smiled. Since she started working here, she'd become used to women who behaved the same way. Many of them frequented this place.

'I'm meeting Fuad here for lunch," Aisha explained, turning to Lami, effectively ignoring Mma.

She stiffened at the mention of the familiar name. Fuad?

No need to panic or get paranoid, she decided. It couldn't be the same person. What were the odds anyway?

Lami's golden-boy brother was too perfect. Not the type to pick a girl from a club, take her home and spend the entire night having mind-blowing sex with her.

"Fuad didn't tell me he was coming here for lunch when I spoke to him a couple of days ago." Lami turned to Mma to enquire. "Do we have a booking for a Fuad Danjuma?"

Mma shook her head slowly. "No, we don't. The only booking is for a Mr Mahmud Danjuma, and he asked for a table for three. He is in the clubhouse now waiting for his guests."

"Okay, Mahmud is my cousin. So that means Fuad is definitely on his way here for lunch." Then, Lami asked quietly, "You say Mahmud is in the clubhouse?"

"Yes, Aunty Lami. The restaurant manager just informed me that he came in a couple of minutes ago. I was on my way to meet him."

Mma was beginning to feel uncomfortable now.

The Fuad from her escapade had been with two friends, Ike and Mahmud. But Fuad Danjuma seemed like a different person from the Fuad she had met in the club. Once again, she told herself not to get paranoid. This was just a coincidence.

She had been so preoccupied with work that she hadn't bothered to glance at the booking for Mahmud's table when it came through.

It would not be the same Fuad.

Smiling, she turned to Aisha, who stared over her shoulder, a huge grin splitting her face.

The first genuine smile from her, Mma thought.

"I can show you to the clubhouse, Ms Aisha," Mma offered just as the revolving doors opened.

Automatically, Mma turned with a smile towards the doors and froze in shock.

It couldn't be.

She was dreaming—had to be. She closed her eyes and opened them again.

Aisha called out a greeting as she walked towards Fuad, who halted in the middle of the foyer, a shocked expression on his face.

Mma took a deep breath and exhaled slowly.

No, she wasn't dreaming. This was real, and she was standing in the reception facing Lami's younger brother, Fuad Danjuma, the same guy from her illicit one-night escapade.

Behind him was Ike, the third friend. There was no doubt about it.

She was doomed.

Oh my God! This was a disaster! A cruel joke from Fate.

She'd had an affair with Fuad 'Eye-candy' Danjuma!

Forcing a smile on her face, she waited by the reception desk with Lami, who had received a call.

Fuad walked towards them, stopping when Aisha met him halfway to hug him.

Mma watched as he bent to give Aisha a peck on the cheek, then he straightened up to walk towards his sister, who had hung up her call and was smiling.

"Fuad, Ya ya dai? You didn't tell me you were coming." She laughed as her brother bent to embrace her. The affectionate love between them was obvious.

He looked down at her, grinning.

"Ike was craving your club sandwich," Fuad explained, shooting Ike a warning glance not to say anything.

"Really, Fuad?" was all Ike said as he came up behind Fuad to give Lami a hug.

Mma noticed that Aisha had quickly tucked her hand into Fuad's, and he made no move to remove it.

She swallowed hard and then turned to look at Ike, who winked and grinned at her.

"I saw that, Ike. Stop winking at Mma! This is Mma, my manager. Mma, my brother, Fuad and his friend, Ike. Fuad, Mma is Ekene's niece. I told you about her, remember?" Lami said, poking Ike hard in the ribs, laughing when he yelped.

Mma glanced at Ike, who in turn was smirking at Fuad.

Then her gaze locked with Fuad's.

"Hello," she said quietly.

His eyes turned hard with anger.

Oh no! Would he say he had met her before? He couldn't! She pleaded with her eyes for him to say nothing about their previous encounter.

As though he understood her, he just shrugged. "Nice to finally meet the famous Mma. Have heard so much about you from Lami and Aunty Ekene."

"Same here," Mma replied, her professionalism kicking into gear.

God must really be on her side today. She offered up a silent prayer of thanks to Him.

To Fuad, she gave a brilliant smile. "Mahmud is in the clubhouse. If you follow me, I will show you to your table. He asked to be put in the VIP section."

She leaned forward and tapped her boss on the shoulder. "See you in a bit."

Lami nodded before waving at them. She disappeared through a side door into her office.

Mma walked briskly toward the lounge with Fuad, Ike and Aisha following.

She sighted Mahmud by the bar and almost wilted in shame when she saw the look of recognition flick across his face. His gaze swung to Fuad and Aisha, and the surprised look on his face was replaced with a mischievous smile.

Men were very predictable. What on earth was he smiling at? Mma wished the floor would open and swallow her. She was wilting from shame. They had to know she had spent that night with Fuad. Why else would they be grinning and throwing mischievous looks at Fuad?

She wondered if he had told them in detail what had happened. Was he a kiss-and-tell guy? And he was engaged too! Ha! She had really messed up this time.

Mma stopped and turned to Ike, looking anywhere but at Fuad. She could feel his anger. She didn't care, and frankly, she wasn't ready to deal with him, especially since he had an overprotective fiancée clinging to his arm.

"I will just get your waiter sorted out." She plastered a professional smile on her face before walking as fast as her legs could carry her towards the kitchen.

She wasn't going back there. Instead, she got one of the waiters to sort out their table and seating arrangements while she used the back door to head back to her office for her meeting with Lami.

She was still in shock.

Fuad Danjuma was Fuad from her one-night escapade.

Mma never thought she would run into him again. As he was Aunty Lami's brother, she wouldn't be able to avoid him. Not good at all.

"Talk about a big mess." She groaned and fell into her seat, her head cradled in her hands. What would they think of her? He and his friends? She didn't want to know, not at all.

All she could think about right now was the amazing night she had spent in his arms. A night she would never forget. A night that would cause her major embarrassment if details of it ever got out.

CHAPTER FIVE

Fuad wasn't surprised that Mma didn't return to sort out their table. He deliberately ignored the questioning looks that Mahmud and Ike were throwing his way and focused on getting through his lunch.

Lami had said the manager was staying in the one-bedroom apartment within the complex. That meant he finally had Mma's address.

Once he dropped off Aisha, who had conveniently left her car and driver at home and come to the restaurant in a taxi, he would head back here to speak to Mma. He mentally prepared for the fight after telling Aisha she could not stay over in his house. Aisha never understood why he would not allow her to spend the night in his place.

Guilt pelted his skin. He'd told her the only woman who would stay over in his house would be his wife. Yet he'd taken a strange woman home. He had allowed Mma to spend the night, and she had taken off by 7am.

Fuad felt insulted. Yes, it had been a one-night stand. But the decent thing would have been to say good morning and goodbye. Well, this evening, they would have the discussion just as soon as he was able to make it through this lunch from hell!

As expected, Aisha threw a fit when she realised she wasn't going to his place to spend the night.

"Why on earth are we having this discussion, Aisha?" He asked quietly. He was angry with her for calling his mother and trying to force him into proposing.

"What do you mean? You have been avoiding my calls for the past two weeks. When I finally see you, you act very coolly towards me. Fuad, do I have to call your mother again?"

At that, Fuad lost his temper.

"Call my mother for what? Aisha? Have you not realised that my mother has no say over how I run my life?" He tried to rein in his temper. He didn't want to hurt her feelings. Still, he wasn't in the mood for a quarrel.

"You know what, Aisha, maybe we need a break from each other to think this through. Please can you get into the car? We are causing a scene here, and frankly speaking, it's embarrassing! So please get into the car!"

Muttering under her breath, Aisha entered the car and slammed the door. Fuad came around and climbed in. Then, without a word, he started the car and drove out of the premises.

Neither spoke until he parked outside her father's massive mansion in Victoria Island.

"I am sorry, Fuad," Aisha began.

Fuad said nothing, annoyance rolling through him.

At Aisha, her mother, and his mum for going behind his back and making plans for his marriage to Aisha.

At Mma for making him feel this way.

But most of all, he was mad at himself for thinking about Mma.

Aisha wasn't giving up, though. She reached out and placed a palm on his arm.

For a moment, Fuad stared at her hand before moving his arm away.

"What exactly are you sorry about, Aisha?"

Fuad was suddenly tired. Sighing, he bent his head and rubbed his temples. His head was pounding, and he couldn't focus. "Can we just leave this discussion for tomorrow? We will talk tomorrow. I can pick you up after work?"

"Fuad?"

"Aisha, please, I will pick you up after work tomorrow. I need to go now, please." He turned to look at her.

Aisha nodded, grabbing her handbag.

"Fuad, sai da safe."

"Sai gobe Aisha," his voice was quiet as Aisha got out of the car.

He smiled at her and drove off.

***

An hour later, he was standing in front of Mma's apartment, his hand on the doorbell. He was about to start knocking when the door swung inward.

She stood there in a pair of shorts and a tee, a frown on her face. At seven in the evening, her workday had ended.

"What?" she began, her eyes widening when she recognised him. Immediately, she tried to slam the door, but he already had a foot in wedging it, stopping her from closing the door.

"We need to talk," was all he said before he pushed past her into her apartment.

Mma slammed the door in anger behind him and stalked after him. 'Talk about what, Fuad?"

"Why did you leave like that without a word?" he swung around to face her.

"You came back here to ask me that?" Mma walked past him, pulling at her long hair.

For a moment, Fuad was distracted as he remembered the feel of her hair between his fingers.

"It was a one-night stand, Oga!" She spoke. "What exactly is the problem? And has it occurred to you that just maybe, that was what I wanted! A night of sex with a stranger no strings attached?"

"Really? That was what you wanted, a one-night stand? Do you go about having one-night stands with men you meet in clubs? I wonder if your Aunty Ekene and my sister know about your other life?" Fuad sneered, staring at her with an incredulous look on his face.

Fuad couldn't believe what he was hearing. She had wanted a night with a stranger. Was she even aware of the dangers of hooking up strangers? She was either naïve or stupid. He couldn't decide which.

More to the point. Why he was angry? He couldn't understand this irritation as if she'd gotten under his skin. It had to be his hurt ego. Why else would he react this way to Mma?

Maybe he was annoyed because he was usually the one walking away when it came to relationships.

But he'd never walked away like she did.

"Look, we had an enjoyable time, and it's in the past. Besides, you are engaged! Why were you picking up ladies in nightclubs anyway?" Mma asked, shrugging.

Fuad smiled.

"I am actually disappointed, you know. Ekene was always talking about you and what an amazing person you are. If only she knew what kind of person you really are," he said, his eyes filled with all the disgust and anger he felt as he shoved his hands into his pockets.

He felt satisfied when he saw her eyes fill with hurt at his comment.

Good, he thought. Let her feel how pained he was. How could she act so nonchalant when his emotions were all over the place, and he couldn't get her out of his thoughts. She was so calm, he decided seconds later, when she schooled her features, looking irritated at the fact that he was here, in her apartment.

"Why are you here? For a repeat performance Fuad? Is that what you really came back for? What are you doing here?"

For a moment, there was silence as they both stared at each other, sizing up each other, then he moved, ambling towards her.

He stopped when he got to her, leaning down to whisper in her ear. "A lame, repeat performance? No, madam, I am not that desperate for a warm body in my bed, and even if I was, it wouldn't be yours. I don't do loose women."

She took a step back, her lips turning in a mocking smile as their eyes met.

"I should be the one saying I don't want a repeat of a lame performance. Did you come here to insult me? Or do you have a valid reason for being in my apartment, Mr Danjuma?" She asked calmly, chin tilted up proudly.

"I really don't know why I even bothered to come here. I guess I wanted to know why you ran off like that," Fuad replied, shrugging his shoulders, still wondering how she could be so calm and composed.

"You know, Fuad, this right here is the reason I do not do relationships. You need to leave now before I call security."

At her last comment, Fuad shoved his hands into his pocket and laughed.

"Really? You, relationships? Have you ever been in a relationship? I was your first, or do you think I would forget the fact that you were a virgin?" His tone mocked her as he raised a questioning eyebrow, "And how would you explain my presence in your apartment considering the fact we just met?"

Mma said nothing and simply watched him.

Fuad could see she was struggling to control her temper, and he smiled inwardly. She looked like she wanted to slap him. Well, she wouldn't be the first.

What was with women slapping him? The thought made him frown.

Mma slid her clenched hands into the pocket of her shorts.

He wanted to reach out, take her in his arms and kiss her until she admitted that she hadn't stopped thinking of him since their night together.

Jeez, but she was hot. Really hot.

Cursing himself for still finding her attractive when she obviously wanted him gone, he shrugged and headed for the exit.

"Have a good evening, Mma," He walked out of her apartment without looking back.

***

Fuad drove straight to Ike's house from the spa.

"What's got you so worked up?" Ike asked quietly after he had handed him a bottle of beer.

"I went to see her."

"See who?"

"Mma, the girl from the club, the manager at The Oasis. Who else would I be talking about?

Ike settled in the armchair opposite, an incredulous look on his face when he finally spoke.

'You went where? Why? Fuad, what's going on? You never go back after a one-night stand, not that you're into one-night stands. But if you do, you just move on! You've never been the clingy kind of guy. Now you are all over the place. Wow, she must have been something else then."

'Ike, we connected. I felt peace just sitting and chatting with her. I like her, but to her, it was just a one-night stand. Can you believe it?" He huffed. "It wouldn't hurt to have a relationship with her, you know?"

"What about Aisha?"

Fuad frowned at his friend. "What about her?"

"Jeez, Fuad!" Ike leaned forward, hands on his knees as he studied his friend. "You need to decide what you want. Either end it with Aisha and go for this babe or forget the babe and stay with Aisha. That's my candid advice."

"I've burned the bridge with the Mma chick, and to her, it was just a one-night stand," Fuad repeated quietly. "I'm messed up, man. The first time I feel something real, it's doomed from the start."

"Something real, eh? So, what do you feel for Aisha, something fake?" Ike enquired, his mouth twisting in a cynical smile. "I swear, there is a loose bolt in that brain of yours."

"Shut up, man. I don't need lectures. I just need someone to talk to."

"Talk to? Do I look like your sister? Look, Fuad, you need to decide what you want to do. Whatever you decide, just know Mahmud, and I got your back, okay?"

For a moment, Fuad stared broodingly at the drink in his hand, then he asked in a subdued voice. "What would you do if you were in my shoes, Ike?"

"Me?" Ike asked.

Fuad nodded, waiting for his answer.

"I would end it with Aisha and ask Mma out. You and Aisha are together because of family pressure, and that's so wrong. She might be beautiful, but she is not your type. I know you don't like Mahmud and I bad-mouthing her, but Aisha is a horrible person, period!"

Fuad said nothing burying his head in his hands.

For the umpteenth time, he wondered why Mma and the whole one-night stand was bothering him so much.

CHAPTER SIX

"Mma, you need to see a doctor," her friend Lola said. Her brows were wrinkled in worry as she lowered her butt next to Mma. She reached out and felt Mma's forehead with the back of her hand.

Mma had a feverish temperature. "I have an appointment at the company clinic. I'm waiting for the driver to come, then we will go. They took blood samples last week. I get the results today."

"What am I here for? Please let's go. I have a couple of hours before I pick Bayo from the office," Lola said, referring to her fiancé.

She got up and held out a hand to Mma, who gave her a grateful smile and stood.

"Thank you, Lola." She smiled weakly. "You are the best."

'Thank me later, madam. Let's get you sorted out first."

***

"What?" Mma stared at the doctor in disbelief.

She looked down again at her blood and urine tests results and read the bold letters on the sheet. POSITIVE.

She looked up in confusion.

"I don't understand." Her voice was calm, but she could hear a roaring sound in her ears. Her head felt like it was about to explode.

This had to be a mistake. The doctor must have mixed up her test results.

"Your tests results came back, Ms Nwachukwu. You are pregnant," The medic repeated gently, watching as Mma gripped the table hard.

She was pregnant? From a one-night stand? With Fuad Danjuma?

"I can't be. It must be a mistake," whispered Mma as she turned to look at Lola, who had accompanied her.

Lola reached over to hold her hand. "Relax, Mma."

Mma shook her head slowly, looking from the doctor to Lola in confusion.

"Did you hear what the doctor just said? Lola, I am pregnant!" She pulled her hand from Lola to clasp her hands in her laps. "Pregnant! Oh my God!"

Staring at the physician in shock, she opened her mouth to speak. Nothing came out. Tears filled her eyes.

This was a disaster. She couldn't be pregnant. Not now.

She choked, unable to breathe, unable to think. Her friend wrapped her arms around her as she wept.

***

Mma walked into her apartment and kicked her shoes off.

She had just come from her mother's house.

After receiving the unexpected news, she had asked Lola to drive her straight to her mother's place. She'd needed someone to speak to—she'd needed her mum.

Since she began working for Lami, her mother had ignored her calls and made no attempt to reach out to her. Her mum would refuse to speak to her whenever she visited, remaining in her room till Mma left.

Today had been different, though.

Ginika had ordered Mma out of the house, not even letting her into the building.

There was only one reason her mother would behave like that. Her grandfather was in town. True to character, her mum had acted to please her father.

Mma did not need this today. She did not need to be reminded that she had "supposedly" failed her mum by turning to Aunty Ekene for help.

She had gone to see her mum because she had found out she was four weeks pregnant and needed her advice, but her mum had turned her away.

Tears slid down her face as she sat on her sofa.

Lola settled beside her and gathered Mma into her arms as she wept.

"It's okay," Lola comforted her. "Look at it this way. You have been blessed with a gift."

But Mma only cried harder. How could she have gotten pregnant the first time she had sex? And Fuad had used protection. He had made sure of it. So how on earth had she become pregnant? Four ~eeks ago, she was happy, with a new job, a new apartment ready to take on the world. And one stupid mistake was going to cost her all of it?

How was she going to explain her pregnancy to Aunty Ekene, to Aunty Lami? They all knew she wasn't in a relationship. So how could she tell her aunties and her sisters about the pregnancy resulting from a one-night stand? Or reveal the father of her baby as Fuad Danjuma?

Fuad Danjuma, who had recently announced his engagement to Aisha Bako.

This was turning into a nightmare. The tears came faster as she realised the mess she had gotten into. She had to think. One thing was sure, though. She was keeping the baby, and she was going to see Fuad.

Wiping her tears, she sat up, her mind made up. It was time she returned Fuad's visit. He was going to be a father, and she needed to let him know.

"I am going to see Fuad Danjuma."

Lola nodded just as Mma's phone rang. Reaching for it, she rolled her eyes when she saw it was Kaira.

"Hey," she answered on the third ring.

"Are you okay? You sounded really down when you called Kelechi and me," Kaira spoke immediately.

"It's just work, jare. I was tired, and Mummy upset me. I just came from the house, and she wouldn't even let me in. Are we still meeting for dinner tomorrow?" asked Mma, wiping her tears, smiling gratefully at Lola, who handed her a handkerchief.

"Definitely. We were supposed to meet at The Oasis. I've heard a lot about the restaurant in the spa you manage. Kelechi and I are dying to try out their club sandwich. We agreed to meet at 8pm for dinner, and then we stay over at yours?"

"8pm is fine." Then, a thought occurred to Mma. "Can we meet at my apartment instead? Will have them deliver the club sandwiches here?"

There was silence, then Kaira asked quietly.

"Are you okay, sis?"

"I'm just tired but really looking forward to our dinner date. Lola will be here too."

Kaira cheered up and chuckled. "Ah, great! Lola is mad fun! See you, sis."

Kaira blew kisses over the phone as she cut off.

Mma sat still for a while, staring at her phone, then sighed and turned to face Lola. She and Lola had met in university and had remained good friends. They had remained in touch throughout Lola's stay in the United Kingdom, where she had furthered her education. Lola had recently returned to Nigeria a couple of weeks ago.

Her friend had been so supportive. Mma was grateful for her friendship. "Thanks, Sis."

"Anytime," Lola replied, standing and walking towards the kitchen. "Let's get something to eat. I am famished, and you need to eat."

"I have to see Fuad."

Lola by the kitchen door and wagged a finger at her friend. "It's not the end of the world, Mma. Everything will get sorted out. Fuad can wait. First, we eat, then you go and tell lover boy that he is going to be a baby daddy."

***

The headquarters of Danjuma group of companies was in Victoria Island, an imposing building of 5 floors with its own private helipad. The Danjuma's were one of the wealthiest families in Nigeria, with a hand in everything from oil & gas to farming to telecommunications and shipping.

Fuad had taken over as C.E.O when his father passed away two years ago.

The only son of the late Abba Danjuma, Fuad, was well known as a very sharp mind in the business environment. According to tabloids, he was also one of the hottest bachelors on the scene and a notorious playboy.

All that had recently changed when the family announced his engagement to Aisha Bako, the daughter of another wealthy family from the same region.

And Mma was standing in the foyer of the headquarters of Danjuma group, waiting to see Fuad Danjuma, waiting to tell him she was pregnant. She had told the receptionist her name, showing her complimentary and ID card, which showed she worked for his sister Lami. Now she was in the lift going straight to the fifth floor where his office was situated.

The doors opened to show a smartly dressed young man waiting for her.

"Ms Nwachukwu, good afternoon. My name is Abu. If you just come this way, Mr Danjuma will see you now."

His PA, a young man in his early thirties, smiled at her as he led the way to what she assumed was Fuad's office.

***

Fuad sat behind the large desk, talking on the phone. He straightened as soon as Mma walked through the massive glass doors into his office, his ever-faithful PA behind her.

He made an excuse, ending the phone conversation immediately. He would return the call later. "Thank you, Abu."

The man smiled and closed the door as he departed.

Hands in his pocket, Fuad turned his attention to Mma, who didn't meet his gaze.

There was something different about her. He'd almost forgotten how beautiful she was. Today, she was radiant.

He had felt a jolt in his chest when she walked in. She still had an effect on him, and he didn't like it.

What was wrong with him? Right now, all he could think of was reaching for her and kissing her senseless.

Then again, she'd made it clear she wanted nothing to do with him.

In the last month, he had sent flowers and gifts which had been sent back. He even showed up at her workplace and tried to talk her into going out with him, but Mma had been adamant.

Finally admitting defeat, Fuad had given up and agreed to his mother's demands that he and Aisha make their relationship official. Two days ago, his engagement to Aisha Bako had been announced.

And yet he couldn't get Mma Nwachukwu out of his head, his thoughts.

But he was determined to avoid any situation which would tempt him to indulge in his fantasies about Mma now that he was engaged to Aisha.

He cleared his throat. "This is a surprise. How are you? I have to ask, though, what are you doing here?"

"I was hoping we could talk?" Mma replied quietly.

"Talk?" Fuad scoffed. "What for? You rebuffed all my attempts to get to know you. So, what on earth would you want to speak to me about?"

"Fuad, you insulted me the night you came to my house! I was hurt."

"Mma, I apologised. I even sent you flowers! I practically begged you for a date. What more was I supposed to do?"

"And that makes everything alright?" Mma shot back at him, her eyes blazing.

"What?" Fuad began, closing his eyes, trying to rein himself in, to control his temper.

After a couple of seconds, he lifted his lashes and spoke calmly. "I apologised. But that is all in the past now. You work for my sister, so our paths are bound to cross. Can we try to be civil to each other? Why are you here?"

Mma exhaled a deep breath, suddenly looking tired.

"Can I please sit down?" She asked quietly, clutching her handbag.

At her question, Fuad watched her closely. She appeared nervous. He had a feeling if she didn't sit down soon, she would faint. Wondering what was bothering her, he slid his hands into his trouser pocket, a frown on his face. The sooner she said what she had to say and left his office, the better for him. Aisha was on her way to see him, and he certainly didn't want her to meet Mma.

"I am sorry, please have a seat. Forgive my manners," he said gently.

Mma took a seat and took another deep breath. "Fuad, I'm pregnant."

Fuad blinked. For a moment, he was quiet, then he strolled around his desk.

Mma said nothing, looking away when he came to stand before her. If he wasn't so shocked and wound up at her announcement, he would have laughed at her expression.

"What?"

"I'm pregnant," she repeated. Sighing, she buried her head in her hands.

He struggled to compose himself. "Mma? What did you say?"

Her head shot up at the coldness in his voice.

"I am pregnant, Fuad, and it's yours... The baby is yours."

"And you expect me to believe that I am the father!" His composure was shot to shreds. He turned away from her, strode towards his desk and leaned against it, shaking his head in disbelief.

"Why would I lie, Fuad?"

"Hey, I don't know, we had a one-night stand. This may be a ploy to get me to marry you, and how do I know you haven't had any other one-night stands since our unfortunate encounter?"

Mma surged to her feet in anger, knocking over her handbag and a stool in the process.

"I haven't slept with any other person. You are the only person I have slept with, and you were my first! Why on earth would I lie?" She yelled at him.

"I am engaged to be married! Mma, what do you hope to achieve? You think you can just stroll in and tell me that I am going to be a father, and everything will just sort itself out?" Fuad asked angrily. "I just announced my engagement. Why now?"

"I just found out! And as soon as I found out, I came here to see you!"

Fuad could see that she was struggling to hold on to what little patience she had, but he didn't care. She couldn't just walk into his office and announce that she was pregnant and expect him to be calm.

Mma's voice shook as she said, "I thought you should know."

"I don't believe you!" Fuad shouted, more from shock than anger.

Mma didn't answer. She couldn't answer.

Instead, she shook her head slowly, bending to pick her handbag. Then, she straightened and smiled sadly at Fuad.

"I am sorry I came here. I just felt you should know." She waited for him to say something, anything, he didn't.

He just stood there staring at her, hands in his pockets, unsure of what to say.

"I'm sorry," she said again before she turned and walked out of his office.

***

She couldn't cry. No, she wouldn't sob.

She was strong. She had Lola and her sisters who would stand by her.

All she needed to do was reach out to her sisters and Lola, and they would rally around her. She walked briskly towards the lift that would take her downstairs, expecting Fuad to follow her. But he didn't. There, she had her answer. Fuad wasn't interested in being a father. Not through her, anyway.

She had done what she came to do. She had told Fuad he was going to be a father, and that was all that mattered. It was up to him to decide if he wanted to be part of their child's life. If he wanted to be, she would not stop him. The biggest problem was her mother, Aunty Ekene and Aunty Lami. What was she going to tell them? How would she explain that Fuad was responsible for her pregnancy?

She walked briskly across the parking lot, where the company driver waited for her and got into the car. She hoped he wouldn't mention the fact that he had brought her to Fuad's office. What reason would she give for visiting Aunty Lami's brother?

"Where to madam?" The driver asked as she settled into the front seat.

"Home, please," she replied as she reached for her phone.

She would cancel her lunch with Aunty Ekene and cancel her dinner plans with her sisters. She was not in the mood to deal with anybody today, and she needed time to think. She would tell them that an impromptu meeting had come up.

Flicking through her phone book, she dialled Lami Abubakar to inform her that she wasn't feeling too well and taking the day off.

***

Fuad watched from his office window as the car carrying Mma left his office premises. He was still in shock. Her news had knocked him for six. She was pregnant? His mother would kill him with lectures of how irresponsible he was if she ever found out that he had gotten a woman pregnant. And Lami, how would she react? She worshipped the ground Mma walked on, and Mma was also her best friend's niece to make matters worse.

Fuad swore softly under his breath, cursing inwardly.

How could he have been so stupid? He was sure he had used a condom that night. No, correct that: he had used a lot of condoms.

Then he swore.

At some point during the night, he suspected one of the condoms had ripped, but he hadn't investigated. He had simply tossed it in the bin and returned to the room, slipping on a new condom. He remembered that night vividly. He had been so reckless, which was unlike him. Why hadn't she been on the pill anyway?

He closed his eyes in disgust as he remembered that she had been a virgin, but then she could have taken an after-morning pill. Why hadn't she?

Groaning in frustration, he thought of Aisha. How would she take it? He would have to tell her that there was no way he would leave Mma to raise his child alone. He would be involved in his child's life whether she liked it or not.

This was a mess. A big pile waiting to explode, and he hadn't handled it well when Mma had informed him that she was pregnant. He could still picture the hurt on her face when he had remained silent. But what did she expect?

Marriage? Whatever the case, he had to sort this out before it blew up in his face.

He reached for his phone and asked Abu to reschedule all his meetings. Then he grabbed his keys, dialling his sister's number as he left his office.

The phone rang a couple of times before she answered.

"Fuad?"

"Sannu, Lami ... Are you home?"

"No, I'm at the office. I must round off here. Mma went home. She's not feeling too well. Why are you asking?" Lami asked.

"I'm on my way to see you. I'll be there in less than an hour."

'Okay, see you in a bit," his sister replied.

If there was anybody he could confide in, it was his sister.

CHAPTER SEVEN

Her bell must have been ringing for a while, but Mma chose to ignore it.

Whoever it was would go away when she didn't answer. She was curled up in her bed and couldn't be bothered to get up. She was too weak from crying, her head was pounding, and she was not in the mood to entertain any visitors. When she got home, she had managed to change into a t-shirt and curled up in bed and then proceeded to cry her eyes out. That had been two hours ago, and she was still in bed feeling sorry for herself.

The bell began ringing again, and she buried her head under her pillow to block out the sound. Suddenly it stopped ringing stopped and then a couple of seconds later, her phone screen lit up, indicating she had received a message.

Grabbing her phone, she checked the message. It was from an unknown number.

"I'm outside your apartment. Can you please open the door?"

"Who is this?" she texted back.

A reply came back immediately.

"Fuad, please open the door."

She sat up in bed immediately, texting furiously, "What do you want?"

"To talk, and I'm not really a fan of text messages, so please open the door."

"How did you get my number?"

"Lami gave it to me, and she knows about us, and she also knows you are pregnant."

What? Mma blinked in surprise, leaping off the bed in panic. He told Lami? She practically ran through her apartment and yanked the front door open, glaring at the subject of her displeasure.

"You told Aunty Lami? Are you crazy? Why on earth would you do that?"

"Hello to you too. You've been crying," he said, taking in her red and swollen eyes.

Without waiting for an invitation, he walked past her into her apartment. She slammed the door shut and followed him into her living room.

"You told Aunty Lami! Why? Without telling me? It wasn't your place to tell her!"

He turned to face her. "I did, and can you stop screaming? I have a headache."

Mma didn't know whether to cry or laugh. She decided on the latter as she was sure she had no more tears left.

She just collapsed into laughter, and then somehow, the laughter turned to tears.

"You told Aunty Lami, why would you?" She kept repeating. That was all she could think of at this point. How would she face Lami?

"Don't worry. I told her we were in a secret relationship which you broke off because I wasn't ready to commit. I didn't tell her about the one-night stand though I was tempted too, considering how you treated me!"

"And you think that makes it okay? Fuad, you are engaged to be married!"

"You should have thought about that before you came marching into my office and announced that you were pregnant with my child. My engagement to Aisha will be called off. You and I will get married."

Mma wasn't sure she had heard him correctly.

"What was that? What did you say?" she asked, not sure if she had heard correctly.

"I said we are getting married. You and I hitched. Fuad and Mma hitched," he replied.

"You must be crazy. No, scratch that, you are mad! And you have overstayed your welcome. Fuad, you need to leave!" She spat at him angrily.

'I am not going anywhere. Did you really expect me to go ahead and marry Aisha when you are pregnant with my child? If you did, then you really don't know me very well, Mma." He folded his arms, watching her steadily.

He appeared calm. How could he be relaxed under the circumstances?

Suddenly he came towards her. She took a step back and stumbled, but Fuad reached out to steady her, preventing her from falling.

She shook her head, shrugging his hands away, then she moved away quickly so she wouldn't be so close to him.

'No, Fuad. We can't. I can't marry you." She was in a panic now.

Marry him? No way! It wasn't going to work. She moved farther away from him, shaking her head, suddenly feeling very cold.

"Why? Do you think I want any child of mine to be born outside wedlock? I would never allow it. And you? What would you tell your aunty? Your mother?"

"Having a child together is not enough reason to get married, Fuad! It's a very wrong foundation for any marriage?"

"Really?" She could practically feel his disgust and anger, and she cringed from it.

Oh God, why had she told him she was pregnant?

"Really, Mma?" he repeated. "Listen, we are getting married. I just endured one hour of tantrums and insults from Lami regarding my irresponsible behaviour and my seducing of a young and naïve woman! So, if marriage is the solution to this mess, then we are getting married!"

"You shouldn't have told Aunty Lami." Mma was struggling not to cry.

How had her life turned into one big mess?

"You shouldn't have, and my situation is not a mess." Her voice broke, and her eyes filled with tears. "We will not get married."

"Don't worry about Lami tagging you an irresponsible woman. Truth be told, she's happy I am breaking off my engagement to Aisha and getting married to you," he said.

"I am not getting married to you!" She yelled at the top of her voice.

"You should have thought about that before you went about having sex with a stranger! What did you think would happen when you jumped into bed with the first man that spoke to you in a club?" He retorted, not caring that his choice of words sounded hurtful.

She winced and shouted back. "And you should have made sure the condoms you used were of decent quality, you stupid oaf! I am not getting married to you!"

"Oh, you are. You will. Like I said, no child of mine will be born outside wedlock. But, you know, you have a choice."

"Do I?" She frowned, crossing her hands across her chest. "Please tell me, Do I have a choice?"

"Yes, I could marry Aisha, and when you deliver my child, hand the child over to me and disappear. My child will be raised under my roof!"

"Never!"

"That settles it then." He strode towards the front door, stopping only when his hand was on the door handle. "Deal with it, Mma. Tomorrow we will see Aunty Ekene and my Mum, she flew into Lagos today from Kano."

His smile was ruthless.

"Mma, I don't joke about serious issues, and this is a serious one. We might not be getting married for love. But we will get married, and it will be a real marriage in every sense of the word."

He smiled again, and then he left, closing the door behind him.

Mma stood there, shaking her head in disbelief. This could not be happening to her.

Since Lami knew the situation. Then Aunty Ekene would find out very soon and then her mother! Ah, she was in big trouble.

Slowly she sunk to the floor, her arms wrapped around her and wept like her life was over.

***

"Fuad, are you sure about this?" Lami asked an hour later when he appeared on her doorstep in her house in Ikoyi.

Fuad didn't want to be here at all. Uwa was in the living room with his entire family, and they were waiting for him so they could discuss plans for his marriage to Aisha. Yes, they could still discuss his marriage plans, but the bride had changed. Ah, this was a meeting he wanted to avoid.

"Yes, I am. In a way, it's a blessing. I now have a valid reason for not marrying Aisha." He grinned, hugging his sister, who simply glared at him and pushed him away

"Why on earth you got engaged to Aisha Bako is beyond me," Lami hissed as she closed the front door behind him. "You keep letting Uwa push you into relationships that do not make sense. The Bako's are not going to be happy, Fuad."

"Pressure, Lami. It was easier to just give in to Uwa's demands. I was tired of all the lectures about my philandering ways, and courting another woman was a lot of stress," he replied quietly.

"So, you were going to live a life of misery with Aisha. How are you going to break your engagement with her? The relationship between both families will be strained," muttered Lami as they walked towards the kitchen to get drinks for her visitors.

She shook her head. "Fuad, you will be the death of me, I swear. Uwa thinks I always support you. I wish she knew how you always disregard my advice."

His sister was worried. He could understand her concern. But he had bigger fish to fry.

His main problems were explaining his actions to Uwa and getting Mma to the altar.

"Wait, Fuad" His sister stopped him by pulling his arm.

Fuad stopped and looked down at Lami. Of all his sisters, she was his favourite, he couldn't refuse her anything, and he couldn't lie to her either, which was why she was the first person he had talked about Mma.

She would always support him in any decisions he took, even if she was angry with him.

"Lami, what is it? You look worried." Fuad asked gently.

Lami took a deep breath. "I know you are probably marrying Mma because you feel responsible for her, but is there any chance that you might grow to have feelings for her?"

Fuad smiled at his sister.

"I won't lie to you and say I am in love with her. I'm not in love with her. I don't believe in love, but I do like and care about her. We can build on that if she agrees to marry me."

"Nagode. Thank you for being honest. Now let's go and break the news to Uwa. I called Mahmud for support. Have you told him yet?"

Fuad shook his head. "No, I haven't."

He looked down at his sister, a frown marring his forehead.

"What is it?"

Fuad shook his head. "Mma has refused to marry me. I'm afraid I have a lot of grovelling and convincing to do," he replied, thinking of his last conversation with Mma. She had yelled that he was the last person she would marry.

Lami chuckled. "If Mma is anything like her Aunty, then you definitely have a lot of work cut out for you."

Raising an eyebrow, she turned to look at Fuad, who had stopped moving.

"Why are you hesitating? Uwa is in there with the crew. Go ahead. I will join you soon." Lami smiled mischievously.

He mumbled under his breath, causing his sister to burst out laughing at the uneasy look on his face. Fuad, with all his arrogance, always cowered when it came to Uwa. They all did.

Uwa was tough. Nobody wanted to be in her bad books or get a scolding from her. She was known for her sharp tongue and her no-nonsense attitude. Getting a girl pregnant was something that would make the matriarch of the Danjuma clan angry.

"Let's go in together," Fuad said, turning to glare at his sister, who was trying hard not to laugh.

"Meaning? Oh, so now you are afraid of Uwa? Come on, move it! Let's go in. The family awaits." She chuckled, reaching out to grasp Fuad and pull him after her. "This is going to be interesting."

She continued laughing as they walked towards the living room where the Danjuma clan was gathered.

CHAPTER EIGHT

Interesting was an understatement.

There was absolute silence after Fuad had made his announcement.

"I am not getting married to Aisha Bako. I just discovered that the lady I was seeing weeks before I announced my engagement to Aisha is pregnant with my child, and I intend to marry her."

There was absolute silence in the room as everyone turned to Uwa, waiting for her reaction. She was the matriarch of the Danjuma family, and her word was regarded as law.

Uwa was a striking woman. All her children had inherited her good looks and height and her strong personality. Of all her children, Fuad was the one that resembled her most in looks and character, which was why they constantly butted heads.

Everyone was waiting with bated breaths to see how Uwa would react, but she remained quiet. Instead, she just sat still, watching her son.

"Uwa?" Fuad began quietly, an uneasy note in his voice.

Uwa held up her hand to halt his speech. When she spoke, her voice was hushed. "Fuad, who is this woman who is pregnant for you?"

"Her name is Mma. Mma Nwachukwu."

Surprised, Uwa turned to look at Lami, who was sitting next to his sister, Zahra.

Mahmud was opposite Fuad. The shock was evident on his face as he turned to stare at his cousin, who shook his head at him and mouthed, "Later."

They all turned to Lami when his mother asked, "Lami, is Mma not Ekene's niece? The one that works for you?"

Lami nodded. 'Yes, she is."

Uwa turned back to Fuad. For a moment, she was quiet, then she dropped her head in her hands and started cursing in Hausa.

Fuad walked over to his mother and took the chair next to her.

"I'm sorry, Uwa," he whispered as she looked up at him, her eyes blazing.

"For what, Fuad? Do you know what you have done? What are we going to tell the Bako's because I will not let you turn that young girl into a single mother. If you got her pregnant, then you will do right by her and marry her? How are we going to handle this?"

She turned to look at Lami, then back at Fuad, and his heart broke. Uwa had a disappointed gleam in her eyes, which hurt him a lot.

Fuad would have preferred anger, but disappointment from Uwa was a big blow. Uwa had always been there for her family, for him especially. After his father died and he'd taken over his father's businesses, Uwa had stood by him, supporting him, and guiding him. He wouldn't be where he was without her help.

He had learnt a lot about the importance of family values from his parents. So Uwa's disappointment in him was something he could not bear.

Getting up from his seat, he knelt before her and took her hands in his. "I am so sorry, Uwa. I should not have gotten engaged to Aisha knowing that I didn't want to get married to her."

"No, Fuad, you shouldn't have. How old is this young lady, Mma?" His mother asked

"Mma is twenty-four, Uwa," Lami supplied from across the room, turning to glare at Mahmud, who went into a fit of coughing.

"She is incredibly young, Fuad. I am really disappointed in you. Mma is Ekene's niece. Ekene is practically family. Are you aware that this can destroy the relationship between your sister and Ekene? Why her?"

Fuad shrugged. "It just happened, Uwa. I fell hard for her. Nobody plans these things."

"Well, at least you are man enough to step up and accept your responsibility. You will marry Mma, but you alone will go to Bakos and inform them why you will not marry their daughter. After two years of courtship! Fuad! How could you?" His mother said, shaking her head.

Fuad could see that Uwa was getting angry now, but she still allowed him to hold her hands, so all hope was not lost yet. She hadn't disowned him.

He could hear Mahmud trying hard to hold his laughter. He would deal with him later, the traitor.

"And you?" Uwa turned to Mahmud, making Fuad smile as Mahmud went quiet.

"Uwa?" Mahmud replied with an uneasy look on his face. What had he done now? He hadn't gotten anybody pregnant, had he?

"Uwa?" he repeated.

Uwa turned to look at Mahmud.

He was like a son to her as she had brought him up as her son when his mother, her sister, had passed away, giving birth to him. 'Your wedding is in a couple of months, is there anything I need to know or is Fatima still your intended bride?"

'Ah Uwa, nothing to tell. Fatima is still my wife to be," Mahmud replied, grinning when Fuad gave him a foul look.

'Good, no more surprises," said Uwa, smiling at Mahmud.

Her smile disappeared when she turned back to the kneeling Fuad and tapped his cheek. "Don't worry, I am not going to kill you. We will start making plans for your wedding to Mma, and I intend to meet her soon. You children will not kill me. Lami refused to marry Isah and married someone else, now you? Haba, you children will not kill me."

"Haba, Uwa, don't be like that na." Her youngest daughter, Zahra, got up, followed by Lami and Mahmud. They came to hug their mother.

"It's true. It will cause a lot of bad blood between the Bakos and us, and I do not know how your Uncle Ahmed will take this news. Alhaji Bako is a good friend of your uncle, and he will be outraged. Already, your Uncle Ahmed thinks I pamper you all a lot, especially you, Fuad. Now you have gone and gotten a young girl pregnant," his mother continued speaking as her children retook their seats.

"If Uncle Ahmed wants to maintain the family relationship with Bakos, then he should get Jamilah married to Aisha's brother, Yusuf." Zahra hissed in disgust, referring to Uncle Ahmed's only daughter.

"Zahra!" Uwa shouted, waving a warning finger at her youngest daughter.

"It's true, Uwa, Uncle Ahmed was the one pushing for Fuad to marry Aisha, who I might add is a very horrible person. Thank goodness Fuad isn't going to marry her. None of us liked her, so why are we all acting like Fuad did the unthinkable?" Zahra went on, a defiant look on her face, daring anyone to contradict her, causing Fuad to smile for the first time since he entered the living room,

No one said anything except their mother, who turned to Fuad. "Handle the Bakos carefully. I hope to meet Mma soon."

She turned back to her youngest daughter Zahra.

"And you, that mouth of yours..." she began, then started smiling when Zahra simply stared back with a defiant expression.

Fuad heaved a sigh of relief and got to his feet as his mother stood.

She looked up at Fuad and smiled. "You were expecting me to be really angry?"

Fuad nodded. "You were insistent on my getting married to Aisha."

"That's because you had been dating her for over a year. It was either marriage, or you end the relationship. You choose to marry her ... Let's go and have dinner. We have a lot to discuss and do this week. Mahmud's wedding is almost here. You sort out your issue with Aisha, and then we can get the ball rolling with Mma and her people."

***

Well, that went well, much better than Fuad expected.

Taking out his mobile phone, he strode away from where his mother and sisters were sitting by the pool, chatting, and flicking through albums with Fatima, Mahmud's fiancée. She had arrived an hour ago for dinner.

He scrolled through his contacts for Mma's name and dialled her number. She answered after the phone had rung a couple of times.

"What do you want?" She answered rudely.

"Wow! Tone it down, lady. I just finished speaking to my mother. She wants to meet you."

"No! Fuad, forget I told you about the child, pregnancy, whatever. Just forget it," She sounded panicky. "I'm not ready to meet your mother. I'm not even ready to face Aunty Lami!"

"How far gone are you?" He asked quietly.

"About 5 weeks," Mma muttered.

She didn't have time before she started showing. There was still so much to do.

"Mma, if the child you are carrying is mine, he won't be born out of wedlock," Fuad warned.

"What do you mean if the child I am carrying is yours? I already told you it's yours!" Mma shouted back on the other end of the phone.

"Then, why can't you see marriage would be good for the baby?"

"When I marry, I want it to be for love, Fuad."

On his side of the phone, Fuad closed his eyes and counted to five, then he said quietly, "I don't do love, Mma. I don't believe in it, and Aisha understood that. I am not going to make false promises to you. I like you a lot, and that's all I can offer you now. Please understand that."

"How can you say that? Your sister has an amazing marriage, and from what Aunty Ekene says, your parents loved each other a lot. How can you be so cynical?" asked Mma in a subdued voice.

Fuad shrugged. "So? I do not believe I can fall in love. If we get married, I will respect you. I will never cheat on you. I will definitely care for you, and we would have a very satisfying marriage in every aspect."

"You are talking about sex, right?" Mma said.

"Yes, I love sex, and I didn't hide the fact from you that night, did I?" He sighed, then said in a low tone. "Look, Mma, we can continue arguing. But the fact is that you are pregnant with my baby. If you choose to marry me, you will not lack, and I dare say, you will be happy. If you decide not to, that's fine, but I will play an active role in my child's life, so you decide what you want to do. My mother would like to meet you, though."

"Fuad, give me till tomorrow let me speak to my Aunty and my mother, okay. I will call you in the evening. I really do not want to be rushed into making a hasty decision. Please, all I ask is for time."

"Fine, you do that. We will talk tomorrow," Fuad said and cut the call.

***

Mma stared at the phone in her hand. Sighing, she turned to her sisters and Lola, who watched her.

"Was that Fuad?" Lola asked.

Mma nodded. "His mum wants to meet me."

"So? There is nothing wrong with that. Listen, Mma. If you ask me, accept his proposal," Kelechi was quick to comment. "The issue is how to tell Mummy. Not only are you marrying someone you met through Aunty Lami, but he is also Fulani and Muslim too. Hmm, wahala dey oh."

"Kelechi!" Her twin admonished her, giving her a dirty look.

"What? Mummy will never agree," Kelechi snapped. "Especially with Grandpa around. It is not going to be easy at all!"

"Maybe I could disappear and just have the baby?" Mma offered hopefully.

"And miss out on marrying that hunk? Fuad Danjuma is every girl's dream. Babe, what's the problem?" This time, the question came from Lola.

"I don't love him. When I do marry, I want it to be for love," Mma whispered, her eyes filling with tears. Nowadays, the tears seemed to come readily. All she had to do was blink, and the tears came pouring.

And right now, even if his offer was tempting, marriage to Fuad didn't feel right, especially because she was pregnant.

"I don't want to be stuck in a marriage to a man who only wants to marry me because I am pregnant with his child," she whispered to no one in particular, but Lola heard her.

"But you like this guy, Mma. If you didn't like him, you wouldn't even be considering his offer," Lola pointed out. Her sisters nodded in agreement. "The way I see it, Fuad is stepping up, and I respect him for that. Not many men will do this. Very few men would cancel an engagement to marry someone pregnant with his child. So, my dear, grab the offer with both hands."

"Lola, my mother—" Mma began

Lola cut in, shaking her head. "She will come around eventually. If she doesn't, it's her loss, but I know she will."

"Aunty Ekene will soon be here. Mma, wipe those tears, and please just pretend like you and Fuad are in love and want to get married. She mustn't know about the pregnancy yet, biko," Kaira said, getting up. "When the time is right, and you have made up your mind about what you want to do, we can go and see Mama and Uncle Nnamdi."

Mma nodded, wiping her eyes.

Her sisters and Lola were right about Fuad. She was surprised and impressed that he was determined to do right by her, even if he had acted horribly when she had gone to his office to tell him she was pregnant.

Would marriage to him be so bad?

***

Fuad spent the better part of the night brooding.

His meeting with Aisha hadn't gone well. There had been a lot of screaming and shouting from Aisha and her mother. Eventually, Alhaji Bako had ordered him out of their house. He had barely gotten home when his Uncle Ahmed called him, raining abuses on him and his mother. It was no news that Uncle Ahmed hated his mother.

His uncle had always felt that Uwa had controlled his late father. His late father had been a practising Muslim, but he had allowed his mother to remain a Christian. To add insult to injury, Lami had refused to marry Isah, the son of Uncle Ahmed's business partner and married her long-time boyfriend. He was not a favourite of his uncle.

His uncle blamed his mother for everything, and what had further strained their relationship was his late father's will.

His late father had made his mother the chairperson of Danjuma Group of companies. He willed everything he had to his children and Mahmud. That action did not go down well with Uncle Ahmed, who had expected to inherit his brother's wealth, even though he was wealthy in his own right.

Surprisingly, he was the only one who was against his mother. All his father's siblings and relations had a good relationship with his mother, except his Uncle Ahmed. Uncle Ahmed's actions stemmed from envy, and everyone chose to ignore his complaints about his mother.

Now, Fuad stood with his phone to his ear, listening to his uncle pour out his venom on him, calling him and his mother unprintable names.

He'd had enough. If his mother wanted to continue being cordial with Uncle Ahmed, she could. He was done with his uncle. He didn't owe the man any explanation for calling off his engagement to Aisha Bako. He had only communicated with the man out of respect and because his mother and Lami had insisted he make the call.

"That's enough, Alhaji Ahmed Danjuma." He cut in rudely, stopping his uncle's tirade. "I do not owe you or anybody any explanation about actions I take. I have had enough of you calling me and my Uwa names. It ends now. I am not getting married to your friend's daughter, and that's final. Have a good evening."

With a muttered curse, he cut the call, tossing his phone on a table.

Angrily, he strode through the dining room to his kitchen, where his Togolese cook, an elderly woman who had been with him for three years, was busy making dinner.

"Good evening, Mama Grace," he said, stopping by the kitchen door.

She turned and gave him a dimpled smile. "Good evening, sir. How today?"

"I'm fine. What are you still doing here? You should have left by now" He walked to the fridge, opening it to take out a can of red bull.

"I will close late today. Sir, don't worry." Mama grace continued chopping up peppers.

"Okay, but make sure Aliyu waits for you and takes you home. Let me know before you leave, okay? I will be in my study."

"Yes, sir," She replied, turning to watch him stride out of the kitchen.

Fuad went to his study after grabbing his phone from the bedroom. He placed a call to his PA, informing him of his broken engagement, instructing him to do damage control.

Aisha had friends who worked for tabloids, and he was sure the news of their break-up would be splashed all over the papers and blogs by tomorrow morning.

The next person he should call was his father's younger brother, Ibrahim. Knowing Uncle Ahmed, he would plan to cause division within the family. However, due to the late hour, he would call Ibrahim tomorrow. Sitting at his desk, he tapped WhatsApp and scrolled through his contacts locating Mma's name.

He messaged her. "Hey, how are you holding up?"

He watched the tick turn blue, indicating she had read the message.

Her reply came immediately. "I'm fine and you, how are you?"

"I'm good. I told Aisha about us today."

'Oh?"

He grinned at her answer.

"Just oh?"

"I'm sorry for causing all these issues, Fuad."

'Stop apologising, Mma, it was meant to be. So, am I seeing you tomorrow?"

"Can I stop you?"

"☺ no, you can't."

"See you tomorrow then, good night."

"Take care."

"Thank you and take care of yourself too."

He smiled as he ended the chat.

Chatting with her lifted his spirits a little. He was out of his depth with Mma. With other women, their relationships were defined—no strings. With Aisha, he had known what he was getting into. A marriage devoid of love that he could deal with because he could manage Aisha.

Though marriage to Aisha wouldn't have been so bad. If he wanted to marry more than one wife, he could.

Love had never been a part of his equation with Aisha.

With Mma, it was different. His feelings for her were all over the place. But it was not love. He couldn't deal with all the messy emotions that came with love. Of course, he was insanely attracted to her, but that was it. Oh, he still resented her for walking out on him after their one-night stand. Still, he had enjoyed her company, their conversation.

That was a start. For the hundredth time, Fuad cursed himself for getting into this mess. It was of his own making.

CHAPTER NINE

Fuad picked Mma up by eleven o'clock the next day. He insisted on taking her to breakfast at Eko Hotel & Suites to relax before meeting his mother later.

"Uwa is quite easy-going, and my sisters are wonderful women. You know Lami. Zahra is also genuinely nice. Just relax and be yourself," he said as they got into the car to drive to Lami's house in Ikoyi, where his mother was staying.

"It's easy for you to say. You aren't the one who broke an engagement," she replied in a soft tone. She stared out of the window, waiting for him to start the car. When he didn't, she glanced at him.

The intense way he watched her made her heart slam against her chest. She swallowed as her skin heated. "What?"

"My family have nothing against you. And this situation is not entirely your fault. I am also to blame for this, too … You have decided to go ahead with the wedding, right?"

"Do I have a choice?" She asked, clenched hands on her lap.

"Mma." He leaned over and covered her hands with his. "Relax. We will make this work, and my family will love you, don't worry."

***

In the end, there was nothing to worry about.

Fuad's family welcomed her with open arms, and no mention was made of her pregnancy. Aunty Ekene, who showed up, and Aunty Lami were over the moon. Fuad had asked his family members not to mention her pregnancy for now. The whole family had agreed.

Halfway through lunch, Mahmud brought in his iPad and opened some blogs to show Fuad. Mma and Fuad were trending.

Mma was labelled the gold digger who got between Aisha and her long-time boyfriend, Fuad Danjuma.

Fuad glanced through the websites then handed the iPad to his mother.

She flicked through the blogs and handed the iPad to Zahra. "Deal with this."

Looking at her soon to be family, Mma felt a pang of envy. They were so close, and the love and affection amongst them were visible. Now she understood why Aunty Ekene valued her friendship with the Danjumas. She was treated like family. They were all she had now that her own family wanted nothing to do with her since she had defied her father and married Uncle Lotanna.

Since she discovered she was pregnant, Mma felt a weight lift off her shoulders for the first time.

Yes, she had made the right decision. She was glad she had agreed to marry Fuad. If she hadn't decided, a lot of relationships would have been destroyed.

She lifted her head and caught Fuad staring at her. He smiled, and she smiled back. She had made the right decision.

The next thing was how to deal with her mother and grandfather. She wasn't looking forward to talking to them, but Aunty Ekene had agreed to go with her.

She hoped her mother would see reason and support her. She did not care for her grandfather's thoughts or opinions, and she did not need him either. Aunty Ekene had already reached out to her father's younger brother, Uncle Nnamdi, and he was overjoyed and ready to stand in place of her father.

No, she would be fine. She had nothing to worry about.

***

A week later, Mma and Aunty Ekene went to see her mother.

They had decided to go first. Then, if the visit went well, they would invite Fuad and his family members to meet her mother. Afterwards, they would visit her late father's brothers in Enugu.

One look at Kelechi's face when she opened the front door showed there was going to be trouble.

Her grandfather was still in town. His rage was legendary, and they'd all been victims of his fists in the past.

Mma followed her aunt into the living room, glad they'd come with the mobile police officer her husband insisted accompany them.

Sure, enough her grandfather was sitting on one of the sofas, watching a movie. But, immediately he saw Ekene, he sat up, a scowl on his face.

"What are you doing here?" He spat out.

Mma's mother came out of the kitchen, a smile on her face, which soon faded.

"Ginika, what is she doing here?" Grandfather yelled.

"What are you doing here, Papa? Last time I checked, this was not your house," Ekene retorted, hands on her hips. The woman obviously wasn't afraid of her father.

The old man got to his feet. "How dare you—"

Ekene held up a hand, interrupting him. "I came here to see my sister, so if you excuse me, I will just speak to her and take my leave."

She started to walk away, but her father gripped her hand forcefully and pulled her back.

Mma expected him to strike her any moment. They were used to his anger, his shouting, and tantrums.

However, Aunty Ekene had never tolerated his excesses. She stared down at the hand holding hers, lips twisted in disgust. "Let go of my hand, now."

Mma hurried outside and returned with the police escort. The officer stood quietly, watching and waiting for orders from her aunt.

Her grandfather released his grip on Aunty Ekene's arm immediately he sighted the officer. He took a step back, a scowl on his face and pointed at the exit. "Leave this house this moment!"

Ekene ignored him and walked to her sister. Ginika seemed frozen to the spot at first. Suddenly she stiffened and pointed her finger at the door. "You heard Papa. You both need to leave. You are not welcome in my house."

Ekene looked like she was struggling to keep her anger in check. She slapped her sister's hand away. "Oh, shut up, Ginika. Here I was, thinking you would have received some sense and stop allowing Papa to bully you. But obviously, you haven't, and you have chosen to remain stupid. I have been paying your rent and your father's rent for the past two years! I'm not here to make peace, biko. I am here because of Mma, so please just shut up and listen so I can get the hell out of here!"

"What about her?" Ginika asked angrily. She didn't like the reminder that Ekene had paid her rent.

Mma smiled sadly as she watched her mother struggle to control her emotions. She wished her mother would stand up to her bully father and for once defend her children. Mma also suspected that Ginika behaved the way she did because she felt guilty at the way she had allowed her relationship with Ekene to deteriorate.

"What about her, Ekene?" Ginika repeated, looking from Mma to her sister.

Mma spoke for the first time. "Someone has asked for my hand in marriage, and he would like to come and meet you."

At her announcement, her grandfather turned in his seat to face his daughters and granddaughter and started laughing.

"So now you need us to give you away? Why won't Ekene give you away?" He doubled over in his seat and laughed harder.

Ginika walked around them and settled on a dining chair. "Who is he, and what does he do? I hope it is not one of your aunt's money-miss-road friends?"

Mma saw red. What was wrong with her mother? Why did she always have to see the worst in people? She was tired of all the fights, the quarrels. Her mother had changed in the last couple of years, and it was sad to see.

"As a matter of fact, he is. I am getting married to Fuad Danjuma, Aunty Lami's younger brother." There, she had said it. Let the sky fall and fall it did.

Her mother jumped to her feet, screaming!

"Chineke! Papa, did you hear her! Onye Awusa! God oh, who did I offend?" She rushed at Ekene and grabbed the front of her blouse, slapping her hand on her chest repeatedly. "Ekene, i ga-egbu m! Ekene, you will kill me! In fact, you have killed me, oh!"

She continued screaming as Aunty Ekene struggled to free herself from her sister. The twins came rushing out of the room just as their mother let go of Aunty Ekene and sunk to the floor. She continued screaming and cursing Ekene and Mma in Igbo.

They immediately rushed to her and started trying to calm her down.

"Mma!" her grandfather bellowed.

"Yes. Papa." Mma turned to face him, dreading what was coming. She hoped he wouldn't hit her again because she wasn't about to change her mind about marrying Fuad.

"Mma, you will resign from the job and tell that man you will not be marrying him. You will also move back to this house ... Have I made myself clear?"

Mma's mouth dropped open in shock. "What?"

Ekene marched over and dragged her towards the exit. She stopped before her father, briefly. The two of them eyed each other.

"Mma is going to marry Fuad Danjuma." Ekene's voice was dangerously soft. "And there is not a damn thing you can do about it."

"Over my dead body, who will give her away? You? Lotanna?" Her father sneered, hands on his hips.

"In Igboland, it is the father and his relatives that gives away his daughter. You are neither her father nor his kinsmen. Her father's siblings are alive, and thankfully, Mma was smart enough to keep and maintain a good relationship with them. Ginika's husband and his people could not stand you when he was alive. I couldn't understand why then, but now I do. Uncle Nnamdi and Uncle Ifeanyi have already met with the Danjumas. They are delighted to give Mma's hand away in marriage. Our coming here was to inform Ginika and not you."

She stepped back and looked at her sister, who was still rolling and wailing and chanting curses and proverbs in Igbo.

"Ginika, after all we went through at Papa's hands as children. The constant beatings and curses we endured, you could not protect your own children from him? Your late husband will be turning in his grave. You are a disgrace to women." Ekene spat at her sister in disgust. "On a final note, I won't be paying for a roof over your head and Papa's head any longer. Neither will Mma! Rubbish!"

Tears filled Mma's eyes as she watched everything escalate. She hurt for her mother, who hadn't been able to escape Grandpa's control. She loved her mother, and she missed her smiles. When had all that changed? Her mother had turned from a warm and wonderful woman into this bitter, unhappy woman determined to make everyone around her miserable.

Gently, Ekene tugged her arm. "We have to leave, Mma."

Her footsteps were heavy as she walked to the car.

"Are you okay?" Ekene asked when they got inside.

Mma nodded, holding back tears. Her aunty reached out and patted her arm. "Your mum will eventually come around. I know my sister. Give her time, okay? Your mum hasn't been a happy woman for a long time."

"And whose fault is that?"

"Just give her time, my dear."

Mma nodded and smiled weakly. "Thank you, aunty, for everything.

Ekene patted her as the driver manoeuvred the car out of Ginika's compound. "Mma, it will all work out in the end."

CHAPTER TEN

Fuad strode to the Eko Hotel pool area. Mahmud and Ike waited there, at their favourite spot.

"I see you have already ordered drinks and food," he said, pulling out the only vacant seat at the table.

"I'm famished. We didn't order food for you, though. We weren't sure how long it would take you to get here," Ike replied, looking over his shoulder and waving at the waiter.

"I'll have what you are having," Fuad said, dropping his car keys and phone on the table.

"So, Mma, how is she?" Ike asked after the waiter had taken Fuad's order and walked away.

Fuad leaned back in his seat, studying his two friends.

"She has finally come around," he replied quietly as he popped a nut into his mouth.

"Good for you." Ike smiled.

"Better her than Aisha! Walahi, I still find it hard to believe you were going to marry Aisha!" His cousin had an incredulous expression on his face.

"Why? You never said anything? You were all smiles and hugs whenever we saw her. Talk about hypocrisy!" Ike raised a questioning eyebrow.

Mahmud shrugged. "Fuad was with her, so I had to act nice. Besides, Fuad was okay playing the field, and it kept him happy." He sat up suddenly as if he remembered something. "You are getting married to someone you actually fancy. Are you going to remain faithful to her?"

Ike was aghast as he turned to give Mahmud an incredulous look. "Are you serious Mahmud, you have to ask him that now? Why would you ask that?"

Mahmud shrugged. "It's a question, and yes, I have to ask! My cousin is a player. Come on, Ike. The night his engagement was announced, he was in Eko hotel with Yolanda. His reason: he was drowning his sorrows. This is different. He likes Mma. So?"

They both turned to look at Fuad, who was staring moodily at the pool.

"Are you okay, Fuad?" asked Ike.

For a moment, Fuad said nothing then, he turned and looked at his friends.

"I like her, guys. I think I might really like her; I have never felt this way about a lady before," he told his friends quietly.

"So?" Ike asked. "that's good, right?"

"Yeah, that's good," Mahmud chirped in. "You guys are getting married."

"Because she has no choice." Fuad took a swig from his glass. "What if she ends up hating me? I think the real problem is what if she's not enough to hold my attention span for long?"

His friends said nothing for a while.

"She has a choice," Ike said. "She has chosen to get married to you. You just need to get over your fear of commitment and give this a chance."

"Fear?" Fuad asked, "I am getting married to her. Isn't that enough commitment on my part?"

Ike shook his head. "No, you act like you are only getting married because she is pregnant with your child, but I know you, Fuad. It's the right thing to do and the right time for you to settle down. Still, you need to give this a chance, bro."

"Hey," Mahmud reached over and gave Fuad a pat on the back. "Let's not overthink this, Bro."

Fuad nodded and smiled wryly. He hoped he was doing the right thing and not forcing a girl ten years his junior into a marriage simply because that was the only way he could keep her in his life and in his bed.

"I just feel selfish. I feel like I'm forcing her into marriage simply because it's what I want," he explained. "She's much younger than me."

"You didn't think about that when you were desperate to leave the club that night and get into bed with her, did you?" Mahmud's sarcasm earned a glare from Fuad and a slap on the back from Ike.

"Mahmud!"

Mahmud grinned at Ike, who simply hissed and turned back to Fuad.

"You made the right decision. I'm not saying this because you are my friend. You might be a player, but you are an amazing guy. Maybe Mma might just find a heart beneath all that rubbish you show to the world. I mean, you could have offered her money and gone ahead with your marriage to Aisha, but you didn't."

"True." Mahmud nodded in agreement.

"So, let's drink to your future with Mma," Ike said. "And hope you both find the happiness you deserve. No use worrying, just relax, smile and be happy."

"A toast?" Mahmud glanced from Ike to Fuad.

Ike nodded, reaching for the bottle of wine, and poured wine into three glasses.

"To the future," Mahmud toasted, raising his glass.

"To the future," his friends replied in unison.
***

"So, after the church wedding, we fly to Niger for the traditional Fulani wedding? I'm looking forward to that!" Lola said as the twins strode into Mma's room, carrying water bottles and a plate of fried chicken wings.

They were in Lola's family house in Ikoyi, getting ready for the engagement party. Aunty Lami organised it for Fuad and Mma.

Two days ago, they returned from Enugu after holding a simple Igba Nkwu wedding ceremony. Uncle Nnamdi had insisted that they have a low key one which Mma had agreed to. Fuad had accepted it too but had insisted that they hold a Fulani traditional ceremony. He had warned her it wouldn't be as low key as the one held in Enugu.

Fuad was the Late Abba Danjuma's first son, and his wedding would be celebrated in style.

"A Fulani wedding. Never been to one of those. I am looking forward to it," Kelechi squealed in delight.

"Yes, oh. I am too!" Kaira sighed, rolling her eyes as she handed a bottle of water to Mma.

"Hmm." Lola grinned. "This is going to be so much fun. I'm glad you accepted his proposal Mma." She reached out to tap Mma on the back.

"Like I had a choice!" Mma replied.

"Hey." Her sister Kelechi turned to look at her. "You had a choice, sis, and you made the right one. I respect Fuad for looking out for you and the baby. I heard he took a lot of slack for doing that. It's all over social media. Aisha took him to the cleaners. According to sources, she claims that she was patient and put up with his philandering ways throughout their courtship. Fuad has been silent, ignoring her, though. Now that's what I call maturity."

"Hmm. Fuad has you all swooning at his feet!" Mma hissed as her sisters and Lola all burst into laughter. "You all are supposed to be on my side, you know. I'm your sister. I'm family, not Fuad!"

At her outburst, Lola came to sit next to her and gave her a side hug. "Listen, Sis. I know this is probably not what you wanted out of life but ever heard of the saying, 'when life throws you lemons, you make lemonade?'"

When Mma nodded, Lola continued, "This is the same thing. A one-night stand, pregnancy and the man involved is doing right by you and not out of duty. You told me Fuad asked you out countless times before announcing his engagement to Aisha, right?"

"He did," Mma grumbled as she recalled the many gifts and requests for a date she had turned down. "He was really persistent, and now, we are getting married."

"Mma, this was meant to be. So, get married and make the best of it," Kaira added, coming to sit on the floor before her.

They were right. Mma had to admit, she was surprised that Fuad had insisted on marriage. She was shocked when he called off his wedding to Aisha and announced his engagement to her. The blogs and tabloids had taken her to the cleaners too. Her reputation had been shredded to bits. Still, in everything, Fuad had stood by her, reassuring her that he wasn't under pressure.

She'd had to close her social media accounts because of the abuses she received daily, especially from people who were meant to be her friends.

Lola and her sister were right. She was going to make this work. She looked up just as a knock sounded on the door, and Lola's mother popped her head into the room.

"Fuad is here to pick you, Mma," she announced, smiling at the girls.

"Thanks, Aunty. I'll be down in a couple of minutes," Mma replied.

Taking a deep breath, she got up and smiled at her best friend and sisters.

"Showtime, ladies."

***

The event was in full swing when Fuad and Mma walked into the venue at the Oasis.

Immediately Ike saw them, he sauntered over, beaming a smile.

"Congrats, Bro." Ike thumped Fuad on the shoulder, and both men hugged before Ike turned and hugged Mma. "Congrats, Sis."

"Thank you, Ike," she said with a smile and stepped away.

Fuad held her back. Surprised, she glanced at him, her eyebrows raised questioningly, but he merely grinned at her and pulled her to his side.

Bending down, he whispered, "Stay with me, please?"

"How can I refuse when you ask so nicely?" she replied, smiling when he threw his head back and laughed before dropping a kiss on her forehead.

She had to admit, it felt so natural being with him. Anyone watching them would think that they were the perfect couple, happy and in love.

"You are going to have to let me mingle at some point, you know that, right?" Mma asked as they accepted drinks from ushers who were carrying trays of refreshments.

"I know." he smiled and waved to a couple who raised their glasses to him. "Let me spend as much time as I can with you. We do have to get to know each other."

He chuckled when she rolled her eyes at him. "Hey, it's normal for a newly engaged couple," he added, smiling.

He was lucky, he decided. Not only was she beautiful, but she was a kind-hearted and decent young lady. Way more youthful than him, though. He winced at the ten-year age gap. But Mma was significantly matured, and she was a much better choice than Aisha.

He shuddered inwardly, thinking of Aisha, thanking his stars that he'd had a narrow escape. Truth be told, Mma's pregnancy was a blessing in disguise. It had given him the perfect excuse to call off his engagement to Aisha, and he didn't regret his actions one bit.

Linking his hands through hers, he whispered, "Thank you."

"Thank you? For what?" She looked up at him in confusion.

He stared at their linked hands before meeting her gaze with a smile. "For giving us a chance. For agreeing to wed me."

He lifted their entwined hands and kissed her knuckles.

Butterflies fluttered in Mma's belly and warmth spread through her. She was in big trouble. She was falling for Fuad Danjuma.

Fuad Danjuma, a notorious heartbreaker.

She smiled back at him, her dimples flashing. "You are making an honest woman out of me too," she replied

Just then, Aunty Lami walked up to them and enveloped her in a warm hug. "Welcome to the family."

Mma hugged her back. "Thank you, Aunty."
***

It was a beautiful night, and Mma had an amazing time. She was glad she had agreed to a party when Aunty Ekene and Lami had brought up the idea.

She owed them for their support.

A couple of hours later, it was time for her to leave. After saying her goodbyes, she walked out into the cool night with Fuad.

He spoke into his mobile. When the call ended, he slid his phone into his pocket and grinned at her. "Abdul is bringing the car. He parked down the street as he couldn't find any space to park here."

"Abdul? You got a new driver?" She asked in surprise. His driver's name wasn't Abdul.

Fuad simply shrugged and said nothing about his new driver; instead, he turned fully to her.

"Can we go to my place?" He asked quietly, watching her.

Mma had a feeling he fully expected her to refuse.

She had avoided and turned down all his invitations to his house, giving one excuse or the other. The last time he had asked her to stay over, she had smiled cheekily and told him to wait until they were married. Their wedding was in a couple of weeks, so he could wait, couldn't he?

He had been the perfect gentleman since their engagement had been announced, patient and understanding. Would it hurt to spend an evening with him?

She smiled and said, "Yes, that would be nice."
***

"Thank you, Abdul," Fuad said when they alighted in front of his house minutes later.

Abdul smiled and greeted Mma before disappearing around the side of the house to the quarters that housed the domestic staff.

"Abdul is your new driver. I hired him a couple of days ago," Fuad said.

"Mine?" Mma squeaked in surprise as Fuad took her hand and led her to his parked fleet of cars. That was when she noticed the brand-new Mercedes Benz GLS SUV.

"Your new car. I hope you like it."

Her mouth dropped open in surprise! Her new car! She didn't even know how to drive.

'Mine?" she repeated in surprise

Fuad nodded.

"Do you like it?" He asked again, watching her face for her reaction.

Did she like it? She loved it! She was pleasantly surprised! A car as a gift? Wow!

'I do," she stammered, "I'm surprised, Fuad."

'Why?' he asked. "You shouldn't be. You need a car, and this is my gift to you."

Mma glanced down at the diamond ring that sparkled on the left third finger. He had put it there an hour ago.

She knew from experience that Fuad hated it when she rejected his gifts.

So, she wasn't going to reject this. Instead, she looked up at him, a genuine smile on her face. Then she took a step forward and kissed him on the cheeks.

"Thank you," she whispered.

For a moment, he was still. Then his arms came around her. Turning his head, he kissed her thoroughly on the lips, smiling down into her upturned face.

"You are welcome," he said after a moment, kissing her softly again. Then he took her hand in his and led her into the house.

CHAPTER ELEVEN

Mma sat in her bedroom in Aunty Ekene's house, waiting for her sisters and Lola to come and get her.

She had to admit she looked beautiful. She was glowing, and she looked gorgeous in her Vera Wang wedding gown.

This was her wedding day. By the end of today, she would be Mrs Mma Danjuma.

Tomorrow, after the family thanksgiving in Aunty Ekene's church, she and her family members would fly to Niger, where the second part of the wedding celebrations would take part.

She had to admit, she was excited as she had never attended a wedding in the Northern part of Nigeria.

One week of festivities, Zahra had explained excitedly. The Danjumas had spared no expense and were going all out for Fuad's wedding, typical with wealthy Nigerians.

She turned as the door to her bedroom opened, and Lola walked in, followed by her sisters. They looked amazing in their champagne bridesmaid dresses.

"You look beautiful, Mma," Lola said, walking over to her childhood friend to adjust her veil. "You are glowing."

"Pregnancy blues, Lola," was Mma's wry reply.

"I hear you!' Kaira said, sitting on the bed, admiring her painted fingernails.

Mma smiled, thinking of Fuad. Truth be told, he had been incredible these past few weeks. The perfect gentleman, very attentive and caring. He had also won over her uncles who initially, had been wary of her marrying a Fulani man, a Muslim. Fuad had won them over totally. His mother and sisters had also stepped in when Aunty Lami and Aunty Ekene had told them about her mother and grandfather. Fuad's mother especially had taken her under her wings, assuring her that her mother would eventually come around.

Mrs Danjuma had also hired a wedding planner who had handled all the wedding arrangements.

The week before, Fuad had flown her to Abuja to meet the other members of the family. All his uncles had been present except Uncle Ahmed. They had later run into him when they paid a courtesy visit to the Emir of Minna, who had been in Abuja on official duty.

She was marrying a good man. They might have got off to a rocky start, but Fuad was a good man, one of the decent ones. He was determined to make this marriage work.

If only they were marrying for love, that would have been the icing on the cake. But she couldn't forget the fact that they were only getting married because she was pregnant with his child.

'Your Uncle Nnamdi is waiting to escort you to the church, oh." Aunty Ekene swept in, looking regal in champagne lace.

Her mother had refused to come. So, Uncle Nnamdi and his wife were taking the place of the parents of the bride. Mma was grateful to Aunty Ekene. She and her husband had lodged all her father's brothers and their wives in Eko Hotel & Suites, where the wedding reception would happen.

Mma got up. "Aunty, I don't know how I can ever repay you."

Ekene simply hugged her and rolled her eyes. "Nne m o. Let's go and get married first, you hear. Your Uncle Lotanna is waiting for me with Nkem."

Mma chuckled as she thought of her Aunty Ekene's daughter. Nkem had returned from London for the wedding. She was driving Ekene mad with requests and following her everywhere twenty-four-seven to know about Ekene's boutique. An exasperated Aunty Ekene had told Mma that she couldn't wait for Nkem to return to London.

Mma laughed, hugging her aunt hard. "Let's go. I'm ready, Aunty."

***

She was finally his.

Fuad grinned to himself as he slid the platinum band onto Mma's finger. He looked up and smiled mischievously, leaning over to whisper to her. "No running off at 7am in the morning again."

He grinned and almost laughed when she looked away in embarrassment. She was a timid lady, and he liked that about her. Fuad smiled, turning back to the official, waiting for him to pronounce them man wife.

"You may now kiss the bride."

He saw her freeze in embarrassment at that pronouncement as he lifted her veil and held her chin. Her eyes were wary, and he could see that she was nervous. But he did tell her this was going to be a real marriage, didn't he?

Gathering her in his arms, he smiled as her arms went around his neck for balance, then he bent his head and kissed her lightly on the lips. It was a kiss meant to reassure her, a kiss full of apology and then it was over almost immediately.

He smiled down at her and said, "Mrs Danjuma, friends?"

At his question, her doubtful expression melted.

It might not be a marriage of love, but at least they could be friends.

"Yes, Mr Danjuma. Friends." she smiled back.

***

Mma had to give the wedding planner credit.

The reception hall was stylishly and beautifully done up. The food was delicious, but she was too tired to eat and only had a couple of light snacks. Right now, all she wanted to do was sleep.

She had been on her feet for the better part of today, and they hurt where the shoes pinched. Whoever said pregnancy was easy was lying and should be slapped a thousand times.

"You must be tired. Do you want to go up to our suite and rest for a bit?" Fuad leaned over and whispered. He'd been watching her for most of the day.

Our suite. She liked the sound of that. "Can I?"

He nodded. "Yes, you can. We have had our first dance, cut our cake. So, we can say our goodbyes and rest before we come back down for the evening party."

"How long do I have to rest?" She asked.

"Three hours. It starts at nine. So, we can get here at nine-thirty."

"That's enough for me," Mma said as Fuad got to his feet and held out a hand to her.

She placed her hand in his, and he pulled her up and started walking, pulling her gently behind him.

As they walked through the hall, they stopped to say goodbye to a couple of dignitaries, informing his mother that they were going to change. Mma was grateful for Fuad's support. Her legs felt wooden, and she didn't think she could walk on her own. She was glad they were staying in the Eko hotel for the night. At least she didn't have to walk extremely far.

After the thanksgiving service tomorrow, Uwa was hosting the family to lunch at the family house. Then the entire family flew out to Niger for the second wedding ceremony. A week from today, they would leave for their honeymoon.

Their honeymoon, like this, was a real marriage.

Fuad hadn't told her where they were going. It was a surprise.

As they walked to the lift that would take them to their penthouse suite, where they would spend the night, he pulled her to his side, tucking his arm around her. The wedding planner fussed around them, keeping guests at bay.

Mma was grateful for his support. She was tired and wanted to just put up her aching feet. Out of the corner of her eyes, she sighted her sisters and Lola standing behind the wedding planner. Of course, they would follow to make sure she was okay.

She smiled at them gratefully. In reply, they gave her knowing winks, and Mma burst into laughter.

At the sound of her laughing, Fuad glanced down and froze. He wished he could capture her amusement with a camera. When she smiled, his heart flipped over. This wife of his was delightful.

Swallowing hard, he moved towards the lift just as the doors slid open. Stepping forward, still clasping her hands, he pulled her behind him. "Time to go, Mrs Danjuma."

She followed, still giggling as the doors slid closed.

Fuad reached behind her and pressed the buttons on the panel, selecting their floor number. He leaned against the wall, crossing his hands across his chest, and just stood, watching her as the lift whisked them up to their penthouse suite.

"What are you looking at?" she asked, raising an eyebrow at him.

"You look beautiful. No. You are simply stunning," he replied.

"You don't look too bad yourself," she said and almost punched him when he threw back his head and laughed just as the lift doors slid open into a brightly lit hallway.

He walked ahead and swiped the key card to open the double doors at the end. Then he stepped back to allow her into their honeymoon suite.

"Wow!" she mouthed, entering the beautifully decorated suite. He followed, tossing his phone onto the table.

Mma surveyed the suite, then whirled around to face him. "This is beautiful."

He nodded, leaning against the wall, hands in his pockets, watching her as she walked around the room.

Even though she was tired, she still looked amazing. Her friend, Lola, had removed the train of her gown and taken the veil. Still, she looked stunning in her wedding gown. His eyes dropped to her stomach. She was twelve weeks pregnant, but unless you looked closely, you wouldn't know she was pregnant.

He could see the changes taking place in her body, the curve of her stomach where their baby nestled, safely, the fullness of her breasts. She was glowing, a healthy glow, the kind that came with pregnancy, his sister Lami had told him earlier on.

Pregnancy looked good on his wife. Ah, it felt good to call her that. To think he'd been avoiding getting married and always had an argument with Uwa whenever she mentioned marriage.

Now, all he wanted to do was make love to his wife. But he couldn't, not now because she wasn't ready. He needed to earn her trust first. Clearing his throat, he straightened and walked towards her.

"You came up to rest," his voice was rough as his hands settled on her shoulders. "Let's get you out of this dress."

"I can manage," she began.

He shook his head and swivelled her, his hand already undoing the tiny buttons at the back of her dress.

"I'll do it. Please let me," he said softly when she started to move away from him.

Something in his voice made her stop and relax. She reached behind and lifted her hair out of the way as he slowly undid the tiny row of buttons. His hands rested on her shoulders, and then, he slowly peeled the dress from her body.

Soon she was standing before him in her lace underwear. She still had her back to him as her dress pooled around her feet. Then his arms slid around her stomach, and his hands rested on the slight curve that was beginning to show. Slowly he drew caresses on her stomach as he bent and kissed her behind her ears.

Mma felt her knees buckle, and she suddenly felt warm all over. Heat pooled between her legs.

"Fuad," Her voice came out in a croak as he pressed kisses along her neck and shoulders.

"Don't worry. I'm not doing anything," he whispered as his hands slid up to cup her breasts. They felt heavier in his hands. "Your breasts are fuller, bigger."

"That's because I'm pregnant," she moaned in reply, her hands tightening by her side.

He kissed her neck again and turned her around to face him.

'Let's get you cleaned up and into the bed for some rest." He took her hand and led her to the bathroom.

Mma swallowed hard. This man was mad! He was going to leave her hanging!

She forced a smile on her face when he stepped back and spoke.

"I will wait for you to finish before I use the shower." Then he was gone leaving her alone and craving his touch.

Fuad waited outside while she had her shower. He knew what would have happened if he had followed her into the shower. He was ready to wait till she was comfortable with him before they became intimate again.

He was determined to make this marriage work. He required them to be friends. Even if love was not involved, respect and friendship, and trust were important to him. Mma needed to be comfortable with him.

He looked up as she emerged from the shower, a towel wrapped around her body, and Fuad felt himself go hard.

His new wife was as sexy as hell. He didn't know how long he could last before his control broke. God help him. He was in serious trouble.

"The bath is all yours." She gestured behind her as he got to his feet.

"Thanks, babe."

He winked as he strode past her into the shower, shutting the door firmly behind him. When he finally emerged, Mma was already in bed. He walked over to the other side of the bed and got in beside her. For a moment, there was silence, then Fuad swore under his breath and reached for her.

"Come here," he said, pulling her back against him, so she was snuggled against him, his arm going around to hold her in place. He kissed the back of her neck. "You smell really nice."

"It's lemon," she whispered, her heart beating fast.

"I love it," he said in an equally low tone, kissing her neck, her shoulders. He felt satisfaction when he felt her shudder. So, she wasn't immune to him.

That was a good sign and a start. Suddenly he was looking forward to their honeymoon.

"Go to sleep, babe. Will wake you when it's time to get ready."

His hand tightened around her as he buried his face in the curve of her neck.

Bliss. She could get used to this, Mma thought, as she fell asleep.

***

They arrived at the poolside for the evening party. Their friends cheered as they appeared hand in hand. Fuad laughed when his friend Ike and Mahmud walked up to him and whispered something in his ear, then he smiled at Mma.

"Welcome to the family Sis, I am sure I must have said that a million times." Ike grinned, moving aside when Mahmud came up behind him to pat Fuad on the back.

'Yeah, welcome. Thank you for saving him." Mahmud grinned.

Mma smiled shyly. She wasn't used to such shows of affection.

She murmured her thanks and moved away, but Fuad tugged her back to his side.

Again.

Surprised, she peered up at him, a question in her eyes.

"What now?" she mouthed.

"I like holding your hands," he said softly, looking down at her, grinning when she looked down in embarrassment.

Mma wasn't used to such affectionate displays, but she was determined to change all that because of Fuad. The brief time she had spent with his family, she could see that they were big on affections.

He grew up in a very loving family with each other. However, she was still shy around him, especially when he was very demonstrative with her in public.

"Let's get something to eat," he said.

She nodded, leading the way towards the buffet table set by the pool, smiling at guests who stopped them to say congratulations. Throughout the evening, Fuad remained by her side, holding onto her hand and enquiring if she was okay from time to time. By midnight she was beginning to feel sleepy, so they bade farewell and headed to their suite.

As soon as they got in, she changed and fell into bed.

"Goodnight," she said sleepily.

Fuad stood watching her drift into sleep, then he went to get changed for the night.

Slipping into bed, he reached across and drew her into his arms and settled down for the night.

CHAPTER TWELVE

Niger was different from Lagos. It didn't have all the hustle and bustle of Lagos Mma was used to.

It was different, peaceful. Beautiful.

There was something about Minna that made her feel relaxed. From the dusty roads to the women dressed in brightly coloured outfits and adorned with ornaments. She had never been to the Northern part of Nigeria before, and she was extremely excited. This was an experience for her and one she was looking forward to.

"What do you think about Minna?" Fuad asked as they drove through the town.

For some reason, he wanted her to like his hometown.

"It is beautiful, very peaceful," she replied, looking around in wonder. "It's not Lagos, but it has a unique feel."

The Danjumas lived on an impressive estate that contained at least twenty houses.

Massive structures, with well-maintained gardens and two or three carports each housing luxury cars. As they drove through the estate gate and down the tree-lined road, Fuad explained that the estate belonged to the family and only family members lived within the estate.

"That's Uncle Ahmed's house," he said, pointing to a massive white house with trees lining the driveway that led right up to the front door.

"My father and his brothers built the estate so we could all be within minutes of each other. They also made sure we came home for all the festivities. That was a law. It still is. Holidays are spent here in Minna, especially if you are married to a son." He smiled as though he remembered his childhood. "Holidays around here is always fun. You would love it."

"Wow." Mma's mouth dropped open.

They drove onto a side street that led to another enormous house, the only one on the entire tree-lined street.

"Wow," she repeated. "This is beautiful."

Fuad grinned, pleasure evident on his face. "It is, right? My parent's house. My house is on the next street, but you can access it from my parent's compound."

Mma was looking around in wonder. It had just dawned on her the type of family she had married into. She had been shocked when she and Fuad had arrived at the local Lagos airport and discovered the Danjuma's had their own private jet.

Now this, an entire estate belonging to one family. Talk about being wealthy. This was a family with serious dosh. Panic assailed her, and she broke out in a sweat. Her hands clenched into tight fists as a uniformed guard opened the gate, and they drove into the compound and parked by the other cars.

Fuad noticed the change in her immediately.

"Mma, what is it?" His voice was soft and reassuring as he stared at her.

He reached for her clenched hands and gently loosened her fingers. She was stiff, tensed. She shook her head slowly, a forced smile on her face.

'Mma," he reached for her chin, gazing into her eyes. He noticed immediately that she was nervous. "What is it?"

Her voice shook when she replied, "I'm scared, Fuad?"

"Why?"

"We come from very different backgrounds, our culture, religion," she began.

Fuad stopped her by placing a finger against her lips.

"So, I'm Muslim and Fulani, and you are Igbo and Christian, what about it? And by background, I take it you are referring to my family's wealth because you were okay until you drove into our family estate?"

When she said nothing, he shook his head and said gently. "My family isn't like that, Mma, you know that. You've spent a lot of time with them in the last couple of weeks."

"But Uncle Ahmed?"

"His feelings and thoughts are of no importance and do not matter to me and should not matter to you either. So now we are going to get out of the car. You will walk into your new home and get enough rest because it has been an exceedingly long day, and I know you must be tired."

Mma nodded, a bit relieved that Fuad hadn't waved away her fears but had tried to reassure her. Now all she had to do was concentrate on the wedding ceremonies scheduled to start tomorrow.

***

She hadn't even spent an hour in the Danjuma family house before Zahra, and her other female cousins came for her.

"Time to have your hands and feet designed with henna, and I have just the design to suit you." Zahra pulled a laughing Mma behind her and through to the living room that had been decorated for the festivities.

A couple of hours later, after they were done with the henna painting session, Aunty Lami and a couple of their older female cousins hosted her to a fantastic dinner. Her sisters and Lola had arrived with Aunty Ekene, and they also joined in the festivities.

They were staying in Fuad's own side of the house, and all they could talk of was how beautiful Fuad's home was.

Looking around at members of Fuad's family, Mma finally relaxed. She had nothing to be afraid of. His family members were a lovely bunch, a couple of them were reserved, but they were still courteous.

And her agreeing to an Islamic marriage ceremony had made them happy. They were elated that she was embracing their culture.

'Fuad is here," Zahra whispered in her ear a couple of hours later, and Mma heaved a sigh of relief, glad he was here because she was so tired.

Mma turned towards the door and saw Fuad standing talking with his mother. Then, as though he felt her eyes on him, he turned, and their eyes met. He smiled at her and nodded, indicating it was time to go home.

Mma nodded, glancing shyly at Zahra, who watched their exchange with an amused look on her face.

"I have to go," she explained apologetically as she got to her feet. "Thank you, ladies, for an amazing night. I had so much fun."

"We did too," Zahra said as she got to her feet and hugged her hard, and a couple of the ladies got up to hug her as they all chorused wished her goodnight.

Mma walked over to Fuad, who pulled her to his side as he spoke to his mother.

Mma overhead Zahra whisper to Lami. 'You know, Fuad is probably crazy about that wife of his?"

Just then, Fuad steered her away, and she didn't hear the rest of the conversation.

Was it possible? Was Fuad in love with her?

She wished but no.

This was a marriage of convenience because she was pregnant. The sisters were just overreading the situation.

Still, her heart clenched tight. She wanted Fuad to be crazy in love with her.

***

The Fatihah, Lami explained to her the next day, as they got her ready, was the first in a series of ceremonies that would be held. Then the Kunshi would be held, after which the Kamu, which was the traditional wedding proper, would take place.

The Walimah, the grand reception, would be the final event and the one Zahra and her cousins were looking forward to.

Mma was intrigued.

To be part of a culture different to hers was beautiful. She had grown up, glancing through magazines celebrating Fulani culture, and now she was a part of it.

Yes, she was looking forward to it. She had always been a lover of diverse cultures and traditions. Marrying into one different from hers was something she found exciting.

After the Fatihah, when her dowry was paid, she was led away by her sisters and in-laws to another house in the estate where she was pampered, adorned with perfumes, scented oil, and decorated with lalei and dressed in an amazing outfit.

"You look amazing," Lola said in admiration. "This shade of blue does you justice."

Mma smiled, looking down at her outfit.

Dressed in the rich navy-blue traditional Fulani fabric, Mma looked stunning, especially with the intricate lalei designs on her arms.

She stared at herself in the mirror and said, "I look really amazing."

"You think?" Kelechi asked, coming to stand before her and burst into laughter when her Lola elbowed her in the ribs.

"Aunty Lami is almost here," Kaira announced. "Hmm, nwanne, you look stunning, the perfect Fulani bride."

"Nigeria does have some amazing and beautiful cultures." Kelechi swivelled to look through the window into the courtyard where women were gathered in groups chatting. "The Fulani wedding ceremonies are a delight to attend. We are going for the Kamu ceremony and then the Walimah, right?"

Lola nodded as she waved her hands towards the door.

"Time to go, Ladies. Our parents and Aunties are waiting to escort our bride to the Kamu ceremony." She smiled as she and the twins led Mma out of the room to aunty Lami, who was waiting in the courtyard.

The Kamu ceremony was held in the event hall within the Danjuma Estate.

Aunty Lami explained that her father and his brothers had built it for family members to hold any event there. It saved them the stress of scouting for a venue if any member of the Danjuma clan had a ceremony.

All they had to was inform the family, and the hall was theirs to use.

"My wedding was also held there," Lami explained, smiling as they drove into the massive compound. "I have to leave you here, my dear. Your aunties and your sisters will escort you into the hall for the ceremony."

Smiling at the twins, she waved at Mma's aunties and disappeared into the hall.

***

Minutes later, Mma was escorted into the hall where Fuad and his family awaited her.

The ceremony went off without a hitch. Mma and Fuad were blessed and joined together in peace and harmony.

Fuad was grinning as the final blessings were said, and he reached down to reach for Mma's hand and clasped it in his. He had been stunned when Mma walked in looking resplendent in royal blue, looking like the perfect Fulani bride.

He was marrying a beautiful woman, and that made him happy.

He looked around the hall and frowned.

Uncle Ahmed stood next to his mother, who sat with the wives of the Emir of Minna.

"What's he doing here?" he whispered to Aminu, another of his cousins who was standing next to him. "He declined the invitations we sent. In fact, he said he would be out of the country. Why did he come?"

His uncle laughed at something his mother said, and Fuad's mouth tightened in anger.

"He has to come, to show face. What excuse would he give the Emir and other dignitaries for missing your wedding?" Aminu shrugged nonchalantly, glancing at their uncle. Alhaji Ahmed Danjuma wasn't a favourite amongst his nephews, and it showed.

"Typical," hissed Fuad under his breath as he watched his uncle make his way through the guests, greeting each one and smiling.

This was his wedding day. He wasn't going to let his uncle's presence dampen his mood or spoil his day. Shaking his head in disgust, he nodded at Lami, who came to whisk Mma away to introduce her to the Emir's wives.

He would not allow his uncle to ruin his mood today. He proceeded to mingle with guests who had come for his wedding ceremony.

CHAPTER THIRTEEN

"Why Italy? Mma asked when Fuad showed her a brochure of the hotel they would be staying for their honeymoon.

"You'll love the Amalfi coast," he told her with a lazy grin.

And he was right.

Their hotel, Le Sirenuse, Albergo di Positano, was beautiful.

She was so excited and kept on exclaiming when they were shown to their suite.

"Oh my God! This is amazing!" She rushed to the window and looked towards the coast. "The view from this window is simply spectacular!" She whirled around and ran to Fuad, giving him a hug. "Thank you, Fuad."

He smiled down at her. "My pleasure. Now let's get changed and go down for dinner."

***

The next few days were the best days of Mma's life. Fuad was attentive, and he was the perfect husband. He took her shopping on the Grand Beach, and they had lunch and dinner in cafés on the Amalfi Coast. The highlight of her trip was the boat rides taken to Capri, Ischia and the Grotta dello Smeraldo cave.

Fuad was delighted that she was enjoying herself. He had discovered Positano during one of his many business trips to Italy. He had fallen in love with the quaint village. So, when Mma had agreed to marry him, he arranged to bring her here for one week. From here, they would head to London for another one week before they returned home to Nigeria.

Their last night in Italy, he took her to Sorrento, a town on the northern arm of the Amalfi Coast that was renowned for its beautiful scenery.

They dined in a quaint café in the hotel Fuad had booked them into for the night. Afterwards, they went to their room and sat on the balcony, sipping juice and eating pastries.

"I have had so much fun, Fuad." Mma gazed at the brightly lit coast. There was something about the scenery. It gave her a sense of peace. "I hope we can visit again."

Fuad sat up and held out his hand to her. "Come here."

She glanced at him hesitantly.

"Please, Mma." His voice was so soft, she had to strain to hear him.

Something in his voice pulled at her heartstrings. Placing her glass on the stool next to her, she got up and went over to him. He gently pulled her down until she sat on his lap. He made sure she was comfortable, then wrapped his arms around her and buried his face in the curve of her neck, breathing in her scent.

"Lemons. You smell so nice. You always do, and I love kissing you there. Your neck enthrals me."

He began placing open-mouthed kisses along the curve of her neck and the back of her neck, his arms holding her tight as he kissed the nape of her neck, then bit her ear lobe gently.

Mma went up in flames as she felt his lips on her skin and had to stop herself from moaning. Her hands gripped the arms of his chair hard as he went back to kissing her, pushing down the top of her dress to place kisses along her collarbone.

He pushed her dress down further until she felt the chilly wind on the back of her neck, his hands sliding round to trace circles on her stomach.

"Fuad?" When she managed to speak, it was a strangled whisper.

"Hmm?" He went back to placing little kisses along the curve of her neck, nibbling her ear in the process, adjusting her, so she was flush against him.

He didn't stop. And she didn't want him to stop. She didn't want him to stop at just kissing her.

"What are you doing?" Her voice shook. She was trying ridiculously hard to stop herself from turning her head to kiss him.

"Trying to seduce my super sexy wife."

"Oh." Her heart was beating fast, and she squirmed when he placed a palm over her beating heart. She was sure he could feel it, then he turned her slowly to face him. His eyes were hot with need.

"I am going to kiss you, Mma. Kiss you senseless till you beg me to stop." He traced her lips with his index finger.

"And I promise, you won't beg me to stop." He whispered, bending to claim her mouth in a kiss.

Mma moaned and slid her arms around his neck to kiss him back.

It felt so good. Fuad needed no further encouragement. He took her chin in his hand and deepened the kiss, smiling inwardly as she shuddered. Mma swept her eyes shut as his lips touched hers. Opening her mouth, letting him in, letting him explore as he skilfully coaxed a fiery response from her, his eyes shut as he deepened the kiss.

This was much better than she remembered, than she imagined. Or did it feel different because they were married?

At last, she thought as Fuad continued kissing her, his hands framing her face.

She had been waiting for him to make the first move since their engagement party, but he had never taken it any further other than a few kisses. She still recalled what he had told her the night he had come to her house to ask her, no, tell her she was going to marry him.

"We are definitely getting married, and it is going to be a real marriage in every sense of the word."

Yet, he had been holding back since they got married. She had caught him watching her a few times, and she couldn't understand why. They were married, so what was holding him back?

143

Now, all that mattered was Fuad kissing her and touching her. But she wanted more from him. So much more than a kiss.

She moaned into his mouth, and he deepened the kiss, and suddenly she wanted him to know that she wanted more than a kiss. She wanted all of him. She could feel him still holding back, so she had to make the first move.

She slid her arms down and under his shirt, touching his bare skin, stroking him as she pressed closer, pushing into Fuad. She smiled in satisfaction when his eyes opened and met hers in surprise.

Fuad was lost the moment she did that. He broke the kiss, pressing his head against hers as he looked deep into her eyes.

"Mma," he said as he reached for her hands and held both in his. If he didn't stop now, he wouldn't be able to stop. But he had to know. He had to see if she was on the same page as he was before they went further.

"Look at me, Mma," he said when she averted her gaze.

"Yes," she whispered shyly, looking back at him.

Fuad closed his eyes for a moment, then opened them again. His voice shook when he spoke. "If we continue, I won't stop at just kissing you. I can't. I've been holding myself back because I didn't want to rush you."

His words summed up how she was feeling, and she felt her heart soar with happiness. She had thought that he didn't find her attractive enough.

She pressed a soft kiss to his lips, her eyes shining. "I'm not stopping you, Fuad, am I?" She whispered.

With a groan, Fuad kissed her again, and in moments they were both soaring high with need. He got up, carrying her through the balcony and into the room, not breaking the kiss. Laying her on the bed, he came down beside her and continued kissing her. She shifted as his hands slipped beneath her short sundress and stroked her skin. His hands crept up and cupped her breasts.

Mma squirmed with need, gasping into his mouth. She wasn't wearing any bra, and Fuad moaned when he discovered that fact.

Sitting up, he pulled her dress over her head and tossed it on the floor, leaving her in a pair of white silk panties, which he got rid of very quickly and then got rid of his own clothing.

"You are beautiful."

He said, staring at her as he covered her body with his, kissing her neck, her eyes, her lips. He made love to her like his life depended on it, kissing her everywhere, worshipping her body. By the time he finally joined his body to hers, Mma was ready to go over the edge. He slid his hand between their bodies and grabbed her hand in his as he surged in and out of her, moaning as she raised her hips to meet his thrusts.

"God, you are so hot, Mma. You make me want to lose myself in you and forget everything but you," he murmured against her lips and just like that, he sent her over the edge. He followed moments later, groaning aloud as he shuddered and emptied himself into her.

***

She woke up to find Fuad leaning on his elbow, watching her. "We leave today, right?" She asked as she yawned, stretching.

He nodded, smiling at her. "For London"

"I wish we could stay here forever," she whispered, touching his face.

"Making love?" he teased, grabbing her fingers and kissing her knuckles, his eyes never leaving hers.

"That too," she replied, squealing as he lifted her and rolled her onto him.

"Let's remedy that." He grinned just before he kissed her.

***

They stayed at The Berkeley, London.

"Only the best for you, my darling," Fuad teased her when they checked into their suite in the prestigious hotel four hours later.

They spent the first two days sightseeing.

Fuad showed her the beautiful landmarks in London. She discovered that Fuad loved buying gifts for the women in his family. He included her sisters and her mum on the gift list.

"My mum isn't speaking to me, Fuad. So, she might not accept any of these presents," she pointed out when he brought out his card to pay for the wristwatch he had gotten for her mum.

"Mma, give her time."

'For how long?"

"You married a Fulani man, a Muslim. You are Igbo and a Christian. You forget Nigeria is a country that is big on tribalism and religion, so it's going to take time for her to come around. Give her time."

"Shouldn't my happiness matter? Your mother didn't have any issues with you marrying a Christian and an Igbo girl, did she?"

Fuad smiled and pinched her nose. "You forget my Mum is a Christian. Give your mum some time. When we get back, we will go and see her, okay?"

She nodded, smiling when he leaned down to kiss her on the cheek.

Another thing she was learning and learning fast. Fuad Danjuma was big on personal displays of affection.

She had a lot to get used to with her husband.

CHAPTER FOURTEEN

After the wintry weather they had enjoyed in Italy and London, the heat of Lagos hit Mma like a wave when they got off the plane.

"Ah, back home at last," she gushed in delight. "The heat! After all that cold in Italy and London, the heat is just what I need!"

"I thought you loved the cold. You said it was relaxing." Fuad laughed, pulling her close as she scrunched her nose and shook her head in mock horror.

Sighting his P.A, who was with two airport officials who would see them through customs, so they wouldn't have to join the long queue, he waved at him. One of the perks of being a Danjuma which he took advantage of whenever he travelled back to the country.

He strode briskly towards his assistant. After exchanging greetings, they were led quickly through customs and, in less than an hour, on their way home to Ikoyi.

Mma fell asleep once they got into the car and slept through the entire journey from Ikeja to Ikoyi.

"We are home, babe. Wake up." Fuad nudged her gently. She looked so innocent sleeping. For a moment, he didn't want to wake her.

"I'm so tired," she murmured as she sat up, accepting his help in getting out of the car. "But I'm glad to be home, no place like home."

"I know." His gaze dropped to the slight curve of her stomach. She was beginning to show, and she was glowing with it. He helped her down from the car, and they walked into the house together. Immediately they got into the house, she yawned and turned to him. He simply smiled and kissed the top of her head.

"Go on up to the bedroom while I make sure all our luggage is brought in."

"Thank you." She nodded sleepily and yawned again.

Fuad steered her towards the staircase. He watched as she climbed the steps to the room, watching till she had turned the corner before he strode towards the front door to make sure all their luggage was brought in.

He had some business calls to make then he would join her in bed.

By the time he shut down for the night and went upstairs, Mma was fast asleep. He stood watching her for a moment as she slept. He still wasn't sure of his feelings for her. He more than liked her, and he was very attracted to her. Everything about her captivated him, and he wanted to get to know her better.

Sighing, he went to get ready for bed. Turning off the bedside lamp, he slid in beside her, careful not to wake her up, but she turned immediately and snuggled up to him.

"What took you so long?" she murmured sleepily, reaching up to plant a loud kiss on his lips, then she rested her head on his shoulder and went back to sleep.

***

They spent the next couple of blissful weeks getting to know each other, something they had failed to do the first time they met. Fuad insisted on dropping Mma off at work every day. Lunch hour was spent together. They either had lunch at The Oasis, or they went to a restaurant on the Island.

Mma insisted on cooking most evenings, even though Mama Grace was available. Evenings were spent at home, watching a movie, or playing board games. Mma discovered Fuad was a favourite topic with blogs and tabloids, something she felt uncomfortable about. Still, he assured her, it was all just talk.

They discovered they had the same tastes in music. They both loved art. So Fuad made sure that they got access to any art exhibitions held in Lagos and Abuja. They also loved football but supported different teams. Fuad was a die-hard Arsenal fan, while Mma loved Manchester United.

Life with each other was slowly getting into a routine.

***

When she was twenty weeks pregnant, Fuad informed her they would visit her mother.

Immediately she panicked, tears filling her eyes. "I can't, Fuad. She won't see me."

"She will." Fuad came over to where she sat eating an apple, pulled her up and enveloped her in a hug. "She will." He brushed back her hair, kissing her forehead. "I spoke to the twins. Your sisters say you your grandfather left a couple of weeks ago."

'It doesn't matter. My mum has been terribly angry with me for a long time."

"Mma, she has been asking after you," Fuad said. "And I have told Kelechi and Kaira we would be coming tomorrow." He took a deep breath. "Mma, she's expecting you."

"She is? Are you sure?"

The hopeful look in her eyes as she looked up at him broke him. He hoped to God he wasn't making a mistake.

"She is, and tomorrow we go and visit her. She is your mother, and it's time you both sit and have a talk."

"Are you sure my grandfather has left for Enugu?" his wife asked with a worried expression on her face.

"Yes, he has," Fuad replied, pulling her into a hug. "He left a couple of weeks ago."

***

They pressed the doorbell to her mother's house the next day at precisely 4pm.

Ginika opened the door and stood for a while staring at her pregnant daughter and her new husband.

Mma was an exact replica of her mother, Fuad realised when he came face to face with his mother-in-law for the first time. He had thought Mma was beautiful, but her mother topped the chart of beautiful women. Ginika Nwachukwu was stunning, and she could pass for Mma's elder sister.

None of her daughters was as beautiful as her.

For a moment, mother and daughter stared at each other, then Ginika opened her arms out to her daughter. That was all the encouragement Mma needed. She burst into tears and fell into her mother's arms, muttering, "I'm sorry, Nne."

"Sssh." Her mother hushed her, hugging her hard. "Omalicha m, come in. Stop crying, you hear."

***

After lunch, Fuad excused himself and took Kelechi and Kaira out, leaving Mma and her mother to talk. They needed time alone, and he was prepared to give her enough time to sort things out with her mother.

"Thank you," Kelechi told him when they left the house. "This means a lot to Kaira and me. Mummy has been so angry for years, and my grandfather did not help matters at all."

Fuad smiled at the young girls he had come to accept as sisters.

'If it was up to my mother and me, we would have come here and insisted your sister and mother make up before the wedding. But Aunty Ekene would not have it, so we had to respect her wishes," Fuad explained quietly.

"I'm glad they are talking. It hasn't been the same since Mma left. Mummy misses Mma, but she won't say it," Kaira spoke this time. "She wasn't always like that, so angry at the world. Everything changed a couple of years ago when she wasn't able to afford to send us to school again, but I'm glad things are back to normal now." She turned and looked at Kelechi, and both girls smiled at each other.

"Now all we have to do is, get her and Aunty Ekene talking," chirped in Kelechi, her grin splitting her face.

***

By the time they got back home to pick Mma, Fuad could see that mother and daughter were more comfortable with each other. He walked in behind the twins, who were chattering excitedly and happy that Mma looked relaxed.

"Fuad," Ginika began quietly, but Fuad simply smiled and reached for her hands.

"Please, Ma. Let's forget the past and start afresh. What's important is that you and Mma have reconciled. Now the next thing is to get you and Ekene talking. Your daughters would love that."

'I have wronged Ekene," Ginika said sadly.

"Your sister, Ekene, is a spitfire, but we all know her weak point. So, if it's okay, we can pick you up for lunch whenever you have time, say next weekend?" Fuad asked.

His mother was on her way to London and would be in town in a couple of weeks. It would be a suitable time for both mothers to meet.

"You don't have to ask twice," Ginika said with a smile.

A couple of weeks ago, when she reached out to Fuad, he had been surprised to hear from her, especially as they had never met.

Fuad hadn't told Mma anything at all about the conversation, he wanted to be sure her mother was ready to see her before he started a reconciliation. So, when the twins had narrated how their mother had locked herself in her room and cried for hours, he knew it was time to visit her. So, he was glad when she reached out to him, asking him to come with Mma.

She had also assured him that her father would not be in residence. The old man had departed in anger when he found out she wanted to reconcile with her daughter and sister Ekene.

"I finally realise how I've wronged my daughters, especially Mma and Ekene. I should have done this a long time ago," Ginika had told him over the phone.

"Better late than never, Ma," Fuad had replied quietly.

Looking at how relaxed Ginika looked, Fuad was glad she had reached out and asked to meet him. It meant a lot to Mma, and that was what mattered.

"Thank you, Fuad," she said again as she watched her daughters laughing and hugging each other.

"You are welcome, Ma."
***

Fuad was in bed, reading a book, when Mma walked into their bedroom from the shower.

She had showered and changed into a yellow nightshirt. He sat up smiling as she approached the bed.

"Hey, you," he said, closing the book and putting it on the nightstand. He pulled back the covers and patted her side of the bed.

She ignored him and walked around to his side of the bed, a mischievous smile on her face. Then she got on him and straddled him, looping her arms around his neck.

"Madam." He grinned, rubbing her rounded stomach. "What are you doing?"

"Getting ready to sleep."

"Really? And this is how you intend to sleep?" he asked, grinning.

She said nothing. Instead, she leaned back and took off the nightshirt she was wearing.

Fuad sat up instantly, growing hard when he saw she was stark naked underneath her nightshirt. She tossed her nightie on the floor and turned to him, smiling mischievously.

"What are you doing, Mma?" he stammered, trying to move.

She was sitting on him, and it was driving him mad.

She grinned, pleased that he no longer sounded like his usual cocky self.

She leaned forward and began kissing his eyelids and nose, anywhere she could and smiled to herself in satisfaction when she heard him groan.

Good. She had him where and how she wanted him.

"Mma?" He asked, pushing her away and looked up at her, a questioning look in his eyes

"Hmm," she murmured, leaning forward to kiss him on the lips as his hands caressed her round stomach. "This is me, thanking you for what you did today. Helping me with my Mum," she whispered against his lips, pressing against him as she slid his pyjama top over his head.

'God, Mma,' he said before he kissed her thoroughly, pulling her to settle between his legs. "If this is how you say thank you, then I accept."

'That's what I thought," she muttered, kissing him back

CHAPTER FIFTEEN

Two weeks later, Mma was sitting in her office waiting for Fuad to pick her up for their weekday lunch when her phone beeped. Tapping the screen, she saw it was a message from Fuad.

"Sorry, Babe. Have to cancel lunch today. We can do dinner later ☺."

She frowned when she read the message, He hardly ever cancelled, and when he did, he would always call to let her know.

Frowning, she typed back a reply.

"Are you okay? Is everything okay at work?"

He replied immediately.

"Yes, babe. Just an impromptu meeting with the board members. Just confirmed I will be home a bit late. Sorry, babe. Will make it up to you."

"Okay sweet. See you later. Will just go home from work. Kisses."

She closed her chat, reaching for the intercom to order lunch from the restaurant.

She ordered Ofada Rice and then settled down to finish work. She was wrapped up when the driver arrived to take her home.

"Good evening, ma," Abdul greeted her as she got into the car.

"Evening, Abdul. How are you? Is your Oga home yet?" She asked as he reversed out of the compound and began the journey back to Banana Island.

"No, I am going to pick him up when I drop you off."

Mma nodded and leaned back in her seat, closing her eyes. Her phone beeped almost immediately. Reaching for her phone, she tapped the screen.

It was a WhatsApp message from an unknown number.

Frowning, she clicked on the message, and an image came onto the screen. Mma froze when she saw the photo and caption that followed it. It was an image of Fuad having lunch with Aisha. He was laughing at something she said. The caption read,

Trouble in paradise, already?

It was a recent picture. In fact, it was taken today. Fuad was wearing the outfit he had left the house in. Was this the meeting he had cancelled their lunch date for?

Mma quietly closed her messaging app, her heart beating fast. There had to be an explanation for this, or why else would he be having lunch with his ex? She felt a headache coming on, so she willed herself to be calm. She took a deep breath, and then slowly, her hands curved around her swollen stomach, and she closed her eyes. She was sure there was an explanation for this. She just had to ask him, she told herself.

***

Fuad came home one hour later.

"Hey, you." He leaned over to kiss her on the cheek.

Mma said nothing, watching him as he strode to the table and dropped his keys.

Her voice when she spoke was so calm. She was proud of herself. "Why did you cancel our lunch?"

He swivelled, eyebrows raised at her question. He was already undoing his cufflinks; "I told you, I had a meeting."

Mma closed her eyes, counted to ten, then said quietly, "Why are you lying to me?"

"What?" His eyes widened in surprise at her comment. He had stopped undoing his cufflinks and was frowning at her.

"What did you say?" He repeated when she remained quiet, watching him steadily.

"You heard me clearly, Fuad. I asked why you lied to me."

"Wow, hold up! Where is this coming from?"

She got up and walked over to him. Then, scrolling through her phone, she handed it over to him. He took it and looked down at the image on her phone.

"You were with Aisha. At least be man enough to tell me the truth," she snapped, watching his eyes widen in surprise, then anger and finally disgust as he saw the image.

Shaking his head, he hissed in disgust as he tossed her phone on their bed.

"What's this, Mma? Are you having me followed?"

"You have a nerve asking me that. Someone I don't know sent me that picture! How did they even get my number?"

"And you expect me to believe that? That a stranger sent you a picture of me having lunch with my ex-fiancée?" He sneered, undoing his shirt angrily.

"Why would I lie? What would I gain by lying, Fuad? I got this picture in a message, and I am asking you where you were and why you were with Aisha. I have every right to ask because I am your wife!"

"Right? What rubbish right are you talking about? What I do during business hours has nothing to do with you!"

"Are you serious? A photo of you having lunch with your ex was sent to me from an unknown number, and all you can say is I don't have the right to ask you about it? Why do you think I was sent that picture?"

"You tell me, Mma! I don't know! How did the stranger get your number?"

'Are you seriously expecting me to answer that? Fuad, I don't know! I just got that picture!"

"I don't believe you, Mma," he started undoing his shirt buttons angrily. "And the fact that I married you, albeit because you were pregnant, does not give you the right to question me on my whereabouts or business meetings. Wallahi, Mma, don't go there at all!"

"Oh my God!" Mma threw her hands up in the air. "Why were you with Aisha? Why can't you answer a simple question, Fuad?" Mma was struggling hard not to scream, but she wished she could slap him. "And why did you lie about it?"

"Okay, I admit, I had lunch with Aisha, okay? She came to the restaurant I was having lunch in. I was with my partners, and I let her have lunch with us for old times' sake! I couldn't throw her out when she asked to join us! She happens to be a family friend, in case you have chosen to forget that fact."

"She's your ex Fuad! A bitter ex! Just listen to yourself, Fuad, for old times' sake indeed! You are married, Fuad!" They were both screaming now at the top of their voices.

"Yes, for old times' sake! I was going to marry that lady until you got pregnant for me! She may not have been perfect, but I wronged her by calling off our engagement, so the least I can be, is civil to her when we meet in public!"

"That does not mean you should have lunch in public with your ex, Fuad! Your Ex! Are you for real, Fuad? So, my being pregnant is now an inconvenience, right? If you feel that way, then why did you marry me?" Mma raged. She was so angry she could hit him, but she had to remain calm and logical. Shouting was never the way to solve issues. "So, my being pregnant is an inconvenience? Is that it Fuad?"

"For God's sake Mma, I didn't say that!"

"You implied it!" She was struggling hard not to cry now. She couldn't afford to weep in front of him. She couldn't let him know that he had hurt her terribly with his actions and his words. How on earth had she gone from anger to tears, she wondered.

"You implied it," she repeated woodenly. "And your business partners, Ike and Mahmud, right?"

"What the hell? Does it matter?!"

"It does! Was your lunch meeting with Ike and Mahmud?"

"Yes, it was. Look, you have nothing to be afraid of. I married you, right? I did right by you. Mma. Our baby will have two parents! All that matters is that I respect you and provide for you and our child!"

"You did right by me? Are you listening to yourself? You keep digging us further into this big hole when it is clear you messed up!"

"What the hell?" Fuad suddenly turned and grabbed a pillow from the bed and strode past her towards the door.

Panicked, Mma whirled around to watch him, "Where are you going to?"

He turned back to face her. "To sleep in the guest room."

"Really?"

"Yes, Mma, I don't do nagging, and I can't deal with your childish tantrums right now. This is one of the reasons I don't do emotions or love or whatever you call it! You are letting your emotions get in the way!"

For a moment, they both stared at each other, saying nothing.

All he had to do was explain to her. That was all she was asking for. An explanation, was that too much to ask for? She waited for him to say something, anything, but he just stood there watching her.

"Suit yourself," she said quietly, walking into the en-suite bathroom. She slammed the door behind her.

She came out only when she heard the door to the bedroom close, indicating Fuad had left the room. Climbing into bed, she curled herself under the duvet and cried herself to sleep.

***

The next day was Saturday.

She was glad. It meant she didn't have to wake up early to go to work. Good, because she could pretend to sleep longer so she wouldn't have to deal with Fuad.

She could not believe he had slept in the guest room. He had chosen to walk out instead of sorting out their issues. She was sure that Fuad would not cheat on her. He was the kind that valued his marriage vows.

If only he had explained, they wouldn't have quarrelled.

He came into their room around ten o'clock to shower. She heard him walk across the room and pretended to be asleep, praying he would take the hint and just leave her alone. Instead, he stopped by the bed, and Mma could feel him watching her, but she lay still and squeezed her eyes shut.

"Mma," his voice was soft. "Are you awake?"

Mma kept her eyes shut. She couldn't deal with him now. If she remained this way, he would just leave her alone. She wasn't ready to speak to him. She was still too raw and angry from their argument the night before.

Fuad seemed to know she was awake, though.

He waited a while, watching her, willing her to answer him, but she just kept her eyes shut. Finally, when she didn't open her eyes, he sighed and went to shower.

***

Fuad hadn't slept all night; he had practically spent the better part of the night cursing himself. Cursing Aisha for gate crashing his meeting and refusing to leave. Guilt at how he had treated her had kept him calm and made him accept her request to join them for lunch.

But the fact that someone had sent his wife a picture, deliberately editing it to crop out Ike and Mahmud, was what annoyed him. How had they gotten Mma's number? And why had he panicked when he had seen the picture on her phone.

He had panicked because, from that angle, the picture made him look guilty! Panic had made him lash out at Mma. Groaning, he dropped his head into his hands and let the chilly water from the shower cascade all over him. He had a lot of begging to do. He had seen the tears in her eyes. He had also seen the hurt she had struggled to hide.

He felt rotten.

Mma was awake and waiting to use the shower when he emerged. A towel hung low around his waist. She barely looked at him but mumbled a hasty "Good morning" as she went to walk past him.

He reached out an arm and stopped her from walking past him.

"Mma, wait."

She pulled away. "Please, Fuad, I can't. Not now, please.' Her voice was hoarse from crying, and her eyes felt brittle and hurt her terribly.

"We need to talk."

"We've said all there is to say." She still didn't look at him but turned and walked into the bathroom, closing the door behind her.

***

"Good morning, Ma," Mama Grace greeted her when she emerged from her room a while later. "Oga asked me to serve lunch by the pool. He's waiting for you."

Mma could go back to her room and ask Mama Grace to bring her a tray, or she could go out and eat with Fuad, act civil and mature. Instead, she instructed the woman to get a glass of cranberry juice to the poolside for her.

Then she walked through the wide glass doors to the pool section.

Sure, enough Fuad was waiting for her before he started eating. He got up as she approached the table and pulled out a chair for her.

"Hey," was all he said.

She smiled brightly at him and took the chair he offered.

"Are you okay?" he asked, taking the chair opposite her, watching her.

Mma nodded. Reaching for a plate, she began heaping food on her plate. She looked up and smiled at him.

"I'm just hungry," she said before turning back to focus on filling her plate with food.

He watched her for a while then reached for a plate too. "They delivered your mum's car today."

She looked up and frowned. "Oh, shoot! I forgot. We need to pick her up today to take her to her new place!"

He nodded, watching her.

His mum had postponed her trip and wasn't coming to Lagos as planned. So, he and Mma had gone house shopping during the week and found a lovely 5-bedroom duplex somewhere in old Ikoyi, complete with pool and servant's quarters. He intended to move Mma's Mum and her sisters there. Aunty Ekene had even helped secure the property. She was excited about doing up the house with Mma's mum.

She smiled, reaching over to grip his hand, a smile on her face, but it wasn't her usual sunny smile. "Thank you, Fuad. Mum would be over the moon."

He patted her hand and replied, "Anything for you, babe. Aunty Ekene said she would love to go with us tomorrow when we deliver the car and take her to the new house."

He was still holding her hand.

"Hmm, can't wait to see both of them together" She pulled her hand away from his and continued eating.

CHAPTER SIXTEEN

Fuad wasn't listening to the memo his PA was reading out loud.

His mind was on Mma. It had been a week since they had exchanged words over Aisha. A whole week. He had tried to explain, but she had cut him short each time, not wanting to speak about it.

Oh, she was polite. They had conversations. She did everything right. She smiled at him. She had lunch and dinner with him every day. They had even gone to Ike's birthday dinner the previous evening, where she had played the role of the perfect wife.

In public, she was all smiles, but something had changed. She had gone back into her shell. She had frozen him out, and it was driving him nuts. Fuad was not used to people giving him the cold shoulder. This was a new experience for him.

He missed her. He missed the Mma he had come to know and admire. He missed the Mma, who was always laughing and smiling and eager to try out new things. Three days ago, when he had returned to sleeping in their room, he had seen the surprise on her face before she had masked it with a look of indifference. She'd said a quiet good night and turned her back on him.

Fuad hadn't slept a wink.

He had lain in bed all night, watching Mma sleep, aching to reach for and hold her. He was so used to sleeping and waking up with her in his arms. He couldn't go on like this. He had to make it up to her, but she wasn't giving him a chance. She had frozen him out.

Reaching for his phone, he typed a message to her.

"Hey, what are you doing?"

He watched as the tick turned blue, indicating she had read the message, then waited for a reply.

"Nothing much. I'm at home. I closed from work early, you?"

He typed another message and hit send.

"On my way home. Will be there in 30 minutes."

She replied almost immediately.

"Okay, see you soon."

That was Mma, polite even if she was angry and she was mad at him. Pushing his chair back, he got to his feet, watching his PA stammer in surprise.

"I have to rush somewhere. I will be back in a couple of hours, finish working on the proposal," He threw over his shoulder as he strode out of his office.

He wouldn't last one more day with Mma acting this way towards him. If he had to grovel and beg to see her smile at him, he would.

***

Mma was in their bedroom when he arrived.

He closed the door and leaned against it, hands in pockets, waiting for her to say something, anything at all. Then, when she didn't say anything, he straightened and walked towards her.

"We need to talk."

She said nothing, just kept watching him steadily, a wary look on her face.

"I'm sorry."

She moved then. She got up from their bed and came to stand before him.

"I know you are, and I also know you didn't or rather you wouldn't cheat on me. You are not that kind of man, I hope ... I wish you had just called and explained to me."

"Mma, I...." Fuad began, but Mma stopped him by placing a hand on his arm.

"Let me speak Fuad. You should have just called me and explained. I was upset that somebody sent me a picture, and when I confronted you about it, you turned it on me and made some nasty comments. I didn't choose to get pregnant or to rope you into marriage. You wanted to get married immediately you found out I was pregnant."

He reached out and grabbed her shoulders, then, pulling her towards him, he took her chin in his hands and tilted her face up to his.

"I would have married you otherwise, pregnancy or no pregnancy. Looking back now, I would never have gone ahead to marry Aisha. Truth be told, I would have gone after you until you agreed to date me. The pregnancy was and is a blessing, Mma."

He pulled her into his arms, burying his face in her neck. She smelt so nice. He loved the fact that she had a lovely scent.

"I'm sorry, babe, I really am. Aisha appeared at the restaurant where we were meeting, and when she asked to join us, I couldn't refuse. I should have." He nuzzled her neck

"Please, Mma."

He pleaded when she remained so still within his embrace, her hands by her side.

"Mma," he said again.

He waited for a while. He was about to step back when he felt her arms go around his neck. And that was when he felt her tears on his face

"Oh no, Mma." He groaned when he realised she was crying. "I'm so sorry."

"I know." She sniffled, hiding her face in the crook of his neck. "Don't mind me. Tears come so easy to me. I guess it's pregnancy hormones."

Fuad heaved a sigh of relief. It was okay. They were fine.

He kissed the top of her head and pulled her away from him to look at her tear-stained face. Her eyes were slightly swollen. He realised she'd been crying before he arrived.

His heart broke. He felt so bad, but she hadn't given him a chance to apologise.

"And you just froze me out instead of telling me how you felt," He tried to lighten her mood and cheer her up. "You can't do that. We need to always talk and resolve issues when we have disagreements."

She scrunched her face, squeezing her nose.

"I had to do something to make you feel bad, Fuad."

"And you succeeded," he whispered, pulling her back into his arms. "I missed you so much."

"Ha!" His wife hissed, "You moved out of our room!"

"I came back."

"After three days, I was counting."

"I am sorry." He grinned, that boyish grin she couldn't resist. "I messed up."

"Yes, you did."

"Kiss me?" He asked hopefully, leaning down to press his forehead against hers.

"I thought you'd never ask," she replied, pulling his head down to hers for a kiss.

He kissed her slowly. "I missed you, babe."

"I missed you, too." She said softly. "I love you, Fuad, you know that, right?"

She felt him tense, and she quickly kissed him on the lips again.

"You don't have to say anything. I just wanted you to know how I feel."

Fuad gathered her in his arms and buried his face in the curve of her neck.

He couldn't deal with her love now. He was okay with the sex and their relationship. He wasn't sure if it was love he felt for her. Why couldn't they just leave things the way they were? Her declaration of love would complicate things. His hands shook as he framed her face.

"I care about you, Mma. I respect you. Isn't that enough? I've been honest from the beginning. I don't want to have to lie to you to make you feel better."

Mma shook her head slowly. "I don't want you to make false declarations of love, Fuad."

"I know, and I'm honest with you. Please don't ask for more, Mma, please. Don't ask for what I can't give."

Her eyes filled with tears. He could see the hurt in her eyes, and the last thing he wanted to do was hurt her any further, but he wasn't sure of what he felt for her.

What if she wasn't enough for him? What if the novelty of having her as a wife wore off after she had given birth? What if she suddenly felt like she was in a marriage she hadn't wanted in the first place? The questions terrified him, and he wasn't ready to talk about his feelings for her, not yet.

"Mma," he began, but she placed a finger silencing him.

"Make love to me, Fuad," his wife said.

He didn't need a second invitation.

He gathered her to into his arms and carried her to the bed, kissing her as he went. There was a desperation in his lovemaking that made her cry as though he wanted to make up for not loving her.

Afterwards, he looked down at her, tensing when he saw her tears, groaning. Gently, he kissed the tears away.

"I'm not a good man. Mma, I'm sorry," he whispered as he kissed her forehead.

She turned her head away, ashamed that he had seen her tears. How would she cope knowing he didn't love her as much as she loved him?

And when had she fallen in love with him?
***

She ran into Aisha Bako two weeks later. It was inevitable. The families moved in the same circles, and having married Fuad, she was bound to run into her soon. She had just walked into The Palms in Lekki, where she had gone to get some vitamins and stretch her legs, when she saw Aisha coming out of Double Four restaurant. Immediately she tried to change direction, but Aisha had already seen her.

"Mma," She called out, waving at her as she walked briskly towards Mma, who smiled weakly and turned back to face her.

"How are you?" She said, coming to a stop, before Mma.

Mma stopped, annoyed that she and to stop and speak to Aisha. It was the last thing she wanted to do, but she smiled sweetly at her and said,

"I'm fine Aisha, how are you?"

"I'm doing great, and you? You look so fat! Pregnancy does change people," Aisha replied, looking Mma up and down. "Really fat, but you are glowing, my dear."

Mma glanced down at her stomach, hiding a smile. She looked amazing. She was glowing, and even if she felt fat and looked fat, she certainly wasn't fat. Of course, Fuad didn't see all that. In fact, he worshipped her body, that much she knew because he told her that every night.

At the thought of Fuad, she felt a sharp pain in her chest. Since the night she confessed her feelings and told him she loved him, things had changed. Fuad had become reserved. Yes, he was polite and still his usual charming self. But Mma could tell he was guarded towards her. That was until he came to bed at night, and then he would change.

In the dark, he took her and made love to her like their lives depended on it. It was as though he was desperate to wipe out her declaration of love with his lovemaking. Afterwards, he would hold her in her arms till she slept.

And all through this, he wouldn't say a word.

She wondered if she should say that to Aisha. Would she splutter and die of shock?

She looked back up at Aisha, a smile on her face.

Aisha wanted to be nasty. Well, two could play that game.

"Fat?" She said, "I feel amazing."

Aisha threw back her head and laughed.

"Oh, you, silly girl, pregnancy makes women fat," She taunted, glancing at her watch. "How is Fuad, by the way?"

"He's fine," Mma replied, turning to look towards her driver, who was walking briskly towards her.

"I was with him a couple of weeks ago for lunch," Aisha said sweetly.

Mma glanced back at Aisha.

She was observing her nails, but it was the expression on her face that caught her attention. Aisha was smirking. It was at that moment that Mma realised that she was spoiling for a fight.

And suddenly, she knew Aisha had somehow gotten hold of her number and sent her that message on WhatsApp. Aisha was looking for ways to rub in the fact that she'd had lunch with Fuad.

But she wasn't going to allow Aisha to gloat or even exchange words with her. Mma was going to play the bigger person.

"I know he told me you guys had lunch with Ike and Mahmud," she said and had the satisfaction of seeing Aisha's mouth tighten.

She glanced at her watch, then added brightly, "It was nice to see you, Aisha, but I have to leave."

She took a step back just as her driver appeared by her side.

"Are you ready, Ma?" he asked, after greeting Aisha.

Mma nodded. "I was just about to leave."

Aisha smiled and spat out a torrent of words in Hausa at Mma's driver, who politely nodded his head.

Mma didn't wait to listen to what Aisha had to say, not that she would understand Hausa anyway.

She was suddenly tired, smiling at Aisha, who was still firing questions at her driver. She turned and walked back towards her car, with Abdul following her immediately, leaving Aisha staring after them.

"Oga said to bring you straight to the office. He is waiting for you," Abdul told her as they were driving out of the mall car park.

Mma nodded. "I got his text, Abdul, but please take me home."

"Yes, Ma." nodded Abdul.

Mma nodded and settled back in her seat, closing her eyes as they drove out into the Lagos traffic. She couldn't deal with Fuad, not now. She was tired of the acting, playing the perfect wife in public and coming home to freezing silence later. She was still trying to understand how everything had changed after the honeymoon.

Instead, today, she wasn't up to it and would go home and sleep. She sent Fuad a text telling him she was on her way home. Her phone rang almost immediately, and she answered on the third ring.

"Hey," she said brightly. "How are you?"

"What's up? You are cancelling? We are meeting Mahmud and Fatima for dinner."

"I'm tired. Can you go alone?" She asked.

In his office, Fuad sat up immediately, feeling concerned. "Are you okay? Are you feeling ill?"

"No, I just want to lie down for a while. I am not in the mood for the company this evening. Please, can you explain to Mahmud and Fatima?"

"Really, Mma, you leave it to the last minute to tell me this? Fatima is flying out to London tomorrow, which is why we arranged this dinner."

Mma bent her head, pinching the tip of her nose between her fingers. Suddenly she was tired, and all the pent-up anger she felt came rushing up, and she just snapped.

"No, I'm just tired, Fuad. I can't go to dinner and pretend everything is all sunshine. Then you will go back to ignoring me like you have been doing except at night when you want …." her voice trailed off. She couldn't continue.

There was silence, and then Fuad spoke in a dangerously low tone. "Are you really having this conversation, Mma? Because I am not ready for your childish tantrums, not today. Are you coming for dinner or not?"

"No. I am going home."

"Fine, will see you when I get back," Fuad muttered and cut the call.

Mma was struggling not to cry as she put her phone away. She leaned back and closed her eyes, willing her headache to go away. She turned her face to look outside as the car sped past.

The tears ran slowly down her cheeks, sniffing. She reached into her bag and took out a handkerchief which she used to wipe her tears. It wouldn't do to cry, not in public anyway. She settled back in her seat fully and closed her eyes again, exhausted.

She woke up to screaming just as they were turning into Banana Island Road.

Sitting up in confusion, she frowned, clutching her bag as the car swerved to the right. Suddenly Abdul screamed out in Hausa as he struggled to control the vehicle. Then there was a crash, and suddenly everything went blank.

CHAPTER SEVENTEEN

Fuad was in the middle of a meeting when his PA interrupted him to say his sister was on the phone.

"I'll call her back in an hour," he said, nodding at the man. "I have to round up quickly as I am due to meet Mahmud in an hour."

"She said it's urgent," his assistant repeated calmly, handing Fuad his mobile phone.

Fuad took the phone, eyebrows raised and spoke into it. "Lami...."

"Fuad," Lami cut in. Her voice was shaky.

Fuad stood up immediately, tensed as he heard his sister's voice. She sounded like she was crying.

"Are you okay, Lami?"

"Fuad, it's Mma. Unfortunately, there's been an accident."

***

The thirty minutes it took him to get to Reddington Hospital from his office must have been the longest thirty minutes of his life. To hear from Lami that Mma was involved in an accident had been distressing.

Especially since the last time they had spoken, he had hung up on her.

Fuad had never felt so scared in his life. Lami had kept screaming and crying and unable to talk. Eventually, he had hung up the phone but not before he got the hospital's name.

All he could do was pray that all would be well and that nothing happened to Mma. Lami was waiting outside Mma's room when he got there. Immediately she saw him, she burst into tears and rushed into his arms.

"How bad is it?" Fuad asked, struggling to be calm, even though he feared the worst.

"Very bad. She's unconscious, and there is talk about operating on her to get the baby out."

"No," Fuad stammered. He pushed Lami and took a step back, moving until his back hit the wall.

"No," he repeated as Lami came towards him.

He held up a hand to stop her.

"She's not ready, I'm not ready, not like this, Lami." Fuad sank into the next available seat and buried his head in his hands.

Lami sat next to him and grabbed his hands. "Fuad."

He looked up.

"And Abdul, Is he okay? Please tell me he is," he pleaded as his eyes filled with tears.

Lami nodded. "He's in a much better position than Mma, Fuad we need to act fast; Ike has gone in to speak to the doctor." She looked up. "Oh, here he comes, the doctors too."

Fuad looked up as Ike walked towards him, a couple of doctors walking briskly behind him.

He got to his feet as they stopped before him.

"Mr Danjuma," one of the Doctors said, stepping forward.

Fuad nodded. He couldn't speak. He was struggling not to break down.

They told him Mma was still unconscious. She had to be operated on immediately and delivered of the baby as the baby was distressed.

"Luckily for us, there was no direct impact on her stomach. The injuries she sustained are to her head and her back and legs. One of her legs is severely injured."

Fuad nodded quietly. He still hadn't said anything at all. He was struggling not to shout, not to rage, not to cry. He wanted to sit down and have a good cry, but he couldn't do that.

"Fuad?" Ike asked him, nudging him at the same time.

Fuad turned and looked at Ike.

"Why isn't she awake, Ike?" was all he said quietly, as though the doctor hadn't spoken.

"She will be fine, Fuad," his friend replied.

Fuad sighed. He closed his eyes for a minute, then opening them, he turned fully to look at the doctor.

"Is Dr Okon available?" he asked quietly

The team of doctors nodded.

"Please, can I request that Dr Okon attends to my wife? I know you are also capable of taking care of her, but I know Dr Okon," he added quietly.

"That is not an issue. We already paged Dr Okon as soon as your wife was brought in. She is on her way in," the older doctor replied.

Fuad smiled gratefully at the team of doctors.

"Thank you very much, Sir. Please, anything you must do to save my wife, do it. Please." His voice broke, and his eyes filled with tears as he stepped forward and gripped the doctor's hand. "Please do it."

***

He prayed. He cried.   Then he prayed again. He cursed. He swore. He raged, and then he sobbed again.

He prayed all night. Even when Lami and Ike informed him that Mma had been delivered of a baby girl and the baby had been taken to the neonatal ICU immediately, he didn't respond. Instead, he just kept on praying.

Kaira, Kelechi and Lola arrived with Aunty Ekene and Ginika a couple of hours after Mma went into surgery.

"How is she?" Lola asked Lami after they had all hugged and exchanged pleasantries.

"We are still waiting for the doctor."

"And Fuad, how is he?" Ekene asked her friend.

Lami looked towards her brother, who sat a couple of seats away, his head in his hands.

"Ekene, He's not speaking to anybody. He hasn't even gone to see the baby. She had been moved to ICU and placed in an incubator thirty minutes ago." Lami shook her head slowly as the tears fell unchecked down her cheeks.

"I pray, Mma makes it, Ekene."

"Lami, she will be fine. She is a strong girl. she will pull through." Aunty Ekene comforted her friend as she said a silent prayer for Mma.

***

Dr Okon came out a couple of hours after Fuad's daughter had been delivered.

Fuad shot to his feet.

"How is she?" He asked as his relatives got up and clustered around him.

"We have managed to stop the internal bleeding," she said. "But she is still unconscious, Fuad. The sudden cut-off of blood flow and oxygen to the brain caused her to slip into a coma. We would have had to induce her into a coma to enable her body to heal."

"Induced her into a coma? Why?" asked Lami

Dr Okon took a deep breath and explained. "She had some complications, HELLP syndrome and an irregularity in her heart. That was what caused her to pass out at the scene of the accident. She was due for a check-up this week. Even if the accident hadn't happened, we would have detected it when she came in to see me. She called me this morning complaining of extreme tiredness, headaches and abdominal pains, so I asked her to come in immediately."

"She never told me. I noticed that she had been tired lately, but I put it down to her being pregnant. So, she's still in a coma?" asked Fuad. He was so calm.

His sister turned to look at him. For someone who had spent the last hours crying, he was so calm. Too calm.

"Can't you do something?" asked Fuad again.

"We've done all we can do for now. We just have to wait and see. We have to wait for her body to heal," Dr Okon, said quietly reaching out to hold Fuad.

She had known the Danjumas for over five years. They had become family friends ever since she had performed a major operation on his mother, and she had also become their family physician.

Fuad shook his head. "I don't believe you" He turned towards her room. "I need to see her."

Dr Okon nodded and took a step back, motioning towards the room.

"We can talk more on the way," she said quietly as she and Fuad began walking towards the room.

"Fuad?" Lami began. Fuad stopped but didn't look back.

"Yes, Lami?"

"The baby, can we go and see her?"

There was silence for a while, the Fuad replied.

"I don't care. See her if you want to," he said, and he continued walking towards his wife's room.
***

"She looks really peaceful."

"Fuad, the operation was a success. She bled a little. Thankfully, we were able to stop that."

"Her leg? How bad is it?" Fuad asked, touching his wife's cheek. Her left leg was heavily bandaged from thigh to ankle

"Her leg is severely injured. We had to operate to remove an iron that had cut into her thigh. She will heal, it will take time, but she will heal." Dr Okon reached out and put a hand on his arm. "Have faith, Fuad."

Fuad threw his hands up in the air in exasperation.

"She will heal! You say the operation was a success, then why the hell isn't she awake, Dr Okon?" He whirled round to face the doctor. "Please tell me why she isn't awake! Will she be able to walk again?"

Dr Okon nodded. "She will walk. Please, Fuad, sit down," the doctor replied, using his first name.

"Sit down now, Fuad," she repeated firmly, pulling out a chair next to Mma's bed.

When he sat down, she took the next seat and pulled it up to him. Sitting down, she took his hands in hers. "Mma will be fine. There is nothing to indicate otherwise. We managed to stop any internal bleeding and deliver her of a beautiful daughter, whom you have refused to see. There were a lot of complications, but we have done all we can, but you need to see your daughter."

"I can't bring myself to go and see her."

"You can, and you will," Dr Okon's tone was firm.

She was right, Fuad realised. He had to see his new baby. He had to believe that Mma would be alright. Where was his faith?

"Can I just stay here for a while, then we can go and see her?" he asked.

Dr Okon nodded and got to her feet. "I will wait outside."

Fuad smiled gratefully, staring down at Mma. Then, reaching for her hand, he threaded his fingers through hers, lifting it to kiss her knuckles.

The tears fell as he rubbed her hands.

"I'm sorry, Mma. I'm so sorry for everything," he began and swallowed hard. "I love you, babe, and I am here waiting. You came into my life and took me by surprise. I know you think I married you out of duty, but that's not true. I married you because I really liked you and I wanted to give our baby a happy home. The love came later. How could it not? Mma, life with you is amazing. I don't think I can live without you, without your smile. I even look forward to our little fights."

He paused as the tears continued to fall.

"Please come back to me, babe. Please, let me show you how sorry I am." He got up and leaned over to kiss her on the lips. "Mma…"

His voice broke, and he sat back, placing his head on the bed next to Mma, and he wept.

And then he prayed again, and he spoke to his wife again.

"We have a daughter. Dr Okon said she is beautiful, but I haven't seen her. I can't go and see her. I'm afraid that I will blame her for you being in this position."

He looked up again. After a couple of moments, he reached out again and touched her cheek, the only part of her face that wasn't covered by a bandage or a plaster.

"I love you, babe. Please wake up. Please just open your eyes," he whispered. "I was too scared to tell you how I felt. I wasn't sure you would be enough for me. I have never been able to stay with a woman for more than two months. With Aisha, it was possible because I had women on the side. With you, I couldn't think of anyone but you. I was scared, Mma, scared of loving you. What if we were not enough for each other? I know now I was wrong" His voice broke again. "Mma, I love you. Hell, I fell for you hard, and I didn't know how to handle your love. Please forgive me and come back to me, don't go, please."

He bent his head and kissed her still hand.

And he wept.

***

When he emerged from her room an hour later, he didn't say a word but simply followed Dr Okon to see his daughter.

"She's tiny," he said quietly, studying his daughter, who was in an incubator.

"She will survive, Fuad," Dr Okon explained.

"Will I be able to hold her?" He continued watching his tiny daughter, a sad smile on his face.

"Not yet," Dr Okon replied. "We do have to monitor her for a while."

Fuad nodded.

"I understand," he said quietly. "Is there a place I can pray?"

"You can use my office," the physician replied without hesitating. "Come, I will take you there."

CHAPTER EIGHTEEN

Fuad spent the next couple of days by Mma's bedside.

He would arrive after delegating duties to his PA in the morning, then spend hours by her bed, reading her favourite romance novels to her. Then he would visit his daughter in the ICU ward and pray over her before he returned to Mma's room.

He prayed, he cried, he fought her, anything to get her to speak to him. He refused to listen to family members that said he needed to relax. He only went home early in the morning to take a shower, and then he returned almost immediately.

The only person who could get through to him was Lami.

She came every evening to keep him company and would just sit with him, not speaking when he cried or when he went into a rage at Mma for not talking to him. He had lost a lot of weight too. That wasn't surprising since Fuad wasn't eating.

"Fuad," she said on her third visit. "Kana lafiya?"

"Ina lafiya," Fuad replied. "I am fine, Lami."

"No, you are not. Dan Allah, talk to me," his sister pleaded.

Fuad turned to face Lami. She was shocked at the pain and suffering in her brother's eyes.

"Fuad, please?" she repeated.

"She told me she loved me," He began, his voice devoid of emotion. "What did I do? I pushed her away and treated her like my sex slave, used her for my own satisfaction."

He laughed as the tears fell. "I did all sort of unthinkable things to her, just because I didn't want to admit I was in love with her. She was hurting, but I didn't care as long there was a body to warm my bed at night. We fought on the day of the accident. I cut the call on her."

He buried his head in his hands. "Wallahi, Lami, ba ni da lafiya. What sort of person does that to a woman he loves and who loves him back? I am a horrible person, aren't I?"

"Kai! Shut up!" Lami got and came to hug him. "You made a mistake." She placed her palm on his chest. "But I know you, I know you, Fuad. Mma is different from the kind of woman you normally date, which is why you fought your feelings for her. Don't do this. We need to be strong for when she wakes up."

"Will she even wake up?" Her brother asked brokenly.

Lami nodded, unable to speak as Fuad hugged her and wept.

Fuad sent a silent prayer up to God.

He had never felt this helpless, this broken. He prayed that Mma would regain consciousness. Otherwise, he didn't know what he would do.

***

One week after the accident, Mma regained consciousness.

Fuad was sitting by her bed, his head by her hip, when she woke up. For a moment, she was disoriented, and everything was blurred. Her mouth tasted and felt funny.

Where was she?

She turned slowly and saw Fuad sitting by her bed, his head on the bed by her hip. She tried to speak, but no sound came out, slowly she lifted her shaking hand. Why was her hand shaky? She placed it on Fuad's head and rubbed his hair.

She couldn't speak. Why couldn't she talk?

There was a tube in her mouth, she realised, and her throat was raw. She slowly shook her husband's head and almost jumped out of her skin when his head shot up in surprise. Their eyes met, and his eyes widened in disbelief, shock and finally, surprise.

She couldn't decide which.

"Mma?" He croaked as he shot to his feet.

She frowned and tried to speak again. He looked really lean, like he had lost weight, and he had also grown a beard. And his hair, when was the last time he visited the barbers? She tried to ask all those questions, but Fuad was shouting, running around her room, shouting into the hallway.

And the tube was still in her mouth, making her extremely uncomfortable. Within minutes, her room was filled with people. She recognised aunty Lami and aunty Ekene, Uwa, her mother and her sisters and Lola. What was Lola doing back in

Nigeria? And they were all crying. Why were they crying?

Suddenly she felt tired. Her head was pounding. It felt heavy. She needed to close her eyes for a bit. Maybe when she woke up, they would tell her what all the drama was for. Closing her eyes, she willed herself to sleep, trying to tune out all the voices.

***

When she woke up again, she noticed Fuad across the room sitting by the door, reading a book.

"Fuad," she whispered.

Thank goodness, the tube was out of her mouth, but she still couldn't speak properly, and her vision was blurred. So blurred, it was frustrating. Everything was hazy, and her eyes hurt.

"Fuad," she said again, and this time he turned at her voice.

He got up immediately and crossed the room, coming to sit on her bed. Then he leaned down and kissed her on the forehead, a smile breaking out on his face.

She noticed he had shaved his beard and trimmed his hair.

"Hey, babe," he said, grasping her hands. "How are you feeling?"

Babe. He hadn't called her that in a long time. So, it felt wonderful to hear him use the endearment again.

She grimaced. "Horrible."

He smiled again, leaning to press kisses along her arm.

"Horrible is good, babe, better than anything?"

She closed her eyes as she felt a pain in her head again.

The headache was draining her, and her eyes still hurt, badly too. Finally, she opened her eyes and attempted to sit up, but it took too much effort, and she fell back, her hands going to her stomach.

"Fuad, our baby?" She asked, fearing the worst. She looked up at him, a panicked look in her eyes as she gripped her stomach hard, wincing from the pain.

Fuad grasped her arms. "Stop. You are hurting yourself. You had an operation. We have a beautiful daughter, Mma."

"Oh." Her eyes filled with tears as Fuad gathered her into his arms and enveloped her in a hug.

"I'm so glad you are okay," he whispered as she hugged him back.

"I'm sorry," Mma began, her voice breaking, as she finally recalled their last conversation, but Fuad silenced her with a kiss.

"Don't. Please don't. I have a lot to say to you but let's get you better first, okay?"

She nodded slowly as Fuad lifted her up and put her across his laps. Her hands went around his neck.

"I'm tired," she said. "So tired."

"I know," Fuad replied, leaning back so she could lean on him. "Just rest," he said, rubbing her back.

She nodded sleepily, settling comfortably into his arms. Within minutes she was fast asleep. And that was how Lami found them when she came in with Uwa, and an hour later, Fuad was lying on the bed, fast asleep, with a sleeping Mma cradled in his arms.

Uwa, who stood behind Lami, watched both for a while, then she smiled.

"See your brother. So, the playboy has a romantic bone in him?" Uwa asked in Hausa.

"Kai, Uwa, don't start. Let's wait outside for them." Lami pushed a grinning Uwa out of the room, knowing that Fuad would die of shame if Uwa ever mentioned what she had seen.

***

She was discharged four weeks later.

Dr Okon had insisted on keeping her in the hospital for a couple of weeks to Mma's frustration. She needed to be under observation, she was told. Coupled with her daughter still in hospital, she had to stay until she was given the all-clear to be taken home.

It was easy to convince Fuad to keep Mma in. He wasn't taking chances with her recovery and ignored all her protests about staying in the hospital. A week after she had regained consciousness, Fuad took her to see their daughter.

"She's beautiful," Mma whispered, looking down at their daughter.

Her eyes filled with tears as she looked down at the tiny human being she and Fuad had created.

"She is. Have you decided on a name? I gave you options," asked Fuad as he turned to wheel her back to her room

"Fa'izah," Mma replied immediately. She didn't hesitate as she turned to look up at Fuad. "I like the name Fa'izah."

"Fa'izah is good." Her husband grinned at her as he wheeled her back to her room.

***

When the time finally came for her to go home, Mma was elated. She was glad to leave the hospital, and she got to go home with Fa'izah too. She was extremely excited to be finally going home with her daughter. However, she was upset that she would use a wheelchair for a couple of weeks as her leg needed to fully heal before she even attempted to walk.

"That's frustrating, Fuad," She grumbled as he tucked her into the state of art wheelchair that had been delivered to her room the day before.

"It's just for a while, Mma. Your leg was severely injured, and you have had two operations on it. You need to rest and not put undue pressure on it," He explained patiently.

They left her room and moved towards the lift that would take them downstairs, where aunty Ekene and her mother waited with Fa'izah.

"Kaira said I am lucky to have a leg; can you imagine that?" she grumbled as the doors to the lift slid open, and Fuad wheeled her in and pressed the buttons that would take them to their floor.

Then he crouched down and scrutinised her face. She was trying hard not to cry, her mouth quivering as she held the tears in.

'Mma," he said quietly, kissing her gently on the lips. "You will be fine. We will be fine."

"You think?" her voice shook as he cradled her face in his hands

"I know," he replied, kissing her again. "Let's go home, babe. It's been hell without you, and I am over the moon that you are better and your leg will get better. So don't fret over it, okay?"

She nodded, just as the lift came to a stop and the doors slid open to reveal her mother and aunty Ekene waiting for them in the hallway.

They were holding Fa'izah, her beautiful baby.

She turned and looked up at Fuad, who rewarded her with a smile.

Mma smiled back, and for the first time since she regained consciousness, she felt relieved. Everything would be well. She had a great support network in her family, and that was all that mattered.

She smiled as she held out her arms to her mother, who stepped forward and placed her sleeping daughter in her arms.

Smiling gratefully at her mother, she bent to kiss her daughter. Fuad's daughter.

"Time to go home, Fa'izah," she whispered.
***

She had been home for a week now and was slowly settling into a routine.

Fuad thought to himself, and he was glad for her. She was getting better and slowly gaining her confidence back. Even Fa'izah was also doing great. He should be happy, shouldn't he, he wandered.

Yet he was here, sitting by the pool, feeling sorry for himself, and nursing a glass of juice in his hands as he thought of his wife. Mma was her usual bright and cheerful self once again, and it was killing him. Especially after how he had treated her in the weeks leading up to her accident.

The day after she returned from the hospital, Fuad had moved into the guest room.

His reason—she needed enough space, and he was afraid he would hurt her leg if they slept in the same bed.

She had simply smiled and said nothing.

But he was lying to her and lying to himself. The truth was that he couldn't sleep in the same bed without reaching for her, without touching her, without holding her while he slept.

Yet, memories of how he had treated her made him feel guilty. Now, he knew how he felt about her, but did she still feel the same way about him? After the way he had behaved to her, did she still love him like before?

He wasn't brave enough to find out, so the best thing was to avoid her if necessary until they could talk. He didn't know when that would happen. Sometime in the future, they would have that talk when he was sure she was much better.

Now he was sitting here waiting while Lami and Kaira, who had come to visit, were in the room with Mma, giving her a shower.

That should have been his job. His job was to take care of Mma, not his sister or her sisters.

Still, he was afraid.

Mma hadn't said a word about loving him since after the accident. Instead, she had poured all the love she felt into loving their daughter Fa'izah.

Swearing, he got up and turned around to go in to get his car keys.

He had been doing a lot of that lately. Driving out to hang out with his friends or sit by himself at a bar, nursing a drink. When he should be with his wife, helping her, loving her.

Snatching his car keys, he strode out of the house.

Getting into his car, he drove to Eko Hotel, which had become his favourite hangout and where he could escape to when he wanted to be alone. Ordering a bottle of water, he sat down by the pool and stared broodingly into space, feeling sorry for himself.

He shook his head, an amused smile on his face. He couldn't believe that he, Fuad Danjuma was afraid of his wife.

Shaking his head, he muttered under his breath, reaching for his drink.

Hopefully, by the time he got home, Mma would be asleep. His phone rang, jolting him out of his thoughts. Glancing down, he frowned when he saw it was Ike calling him.

He answered on the third ring. "Hey, Ike."

"Are you stupid?" Ike asked angrily. "What the hell is wrong with you?"

"What?" Fuad sat up. "What the hell, Ike? What on earth are you talking about?"

"Lami just called me! She told me everything. She is so angry. What the hell, man? You should be at home. I know you, Bro, and I know how you think. You need to go home and face your wife, deal with it, Fuad."

"Ike?"

"No, Fuad, go home now," his friend said and then hung up.

***

Lami was waiting in the foyer when Fuad got back.

One look at her face showed she was angry, and he was in for a lecture.

"Where are you coming from, Fuad?" She asked quietly, too quietly.

"I was suddenly craving some Glover Court suya," Fuad replied, nodding towards the paper bag containing the suya he had stopped to buy on his way home.

Mma loved Glover Court suya. "Have you guys finished helping Mma?"

"Finished?" Lami asked, raising a questioning eyebrow. "No. We decided not to do it. You will do it. Kaira left a while ago. I asked her to leave, and I am on my way home. I was waiting for you to return before I leave."

"Hey, Lami—" Fuad began but stopped when his sister took a step forward.

Her hand clenched by her sides, an angry look on her usually friendly face.

Wow, she was pissed.

"What is it, Lami?" he asked warily, stepping back

"Are you stupid, Fuad? What is wrong with you? Do you realise that Mma needs you now more than ever? What the hell is wrong with you? How do you manage to switch your feelings on and off? I thought you said you loved your wife?"

"I do, Lami, but—"

"No buts here. I am heading home now. You can decide to take care of Mma or not. While you are at it, move to the BQ or a hotel, you silly, bumbling idiot!" his sister hissed, turning on her heel and walking back into the house.

"Goodnight!" she threw over her shoulder as she swept through the house.

For a moment, Fuad said nothing, then cursing under his breath, he walked into the house and upstairs to the bedroom he had vacated a couple of days ago. Lami was right. He felt like a fool, a selfish person. What was wrong with him?

He pushed the door to the bedroom and stopped when he saw her.

Mma was sitting on the bed, in a white towel, a dejected look on her face as she stared down at her damaged leg with its jagged scar.

She looked up as he came in, and his heart slammed into his ribs as he saw the hurt, the pain in her eyes. He said nothing even when she smiled sadly at him. Instead, he hurriedly took off the kaftan he was wearing. Then, crossing to her, he lifted her up, towel and all into his arms.

Her arms went around his neck instinctively.

"Fuad?"

"Shh, let's get you all cleaned up and ready for bed," he said, pulling off the towel as they stepped into the shower together. Setting her gently on the seat provided for her in the shower, he proceeded to wash her gently.

Minutes later, he wrapped her in a towel, carried her through to the bedroom, and placed her on the bed. Then wiped himself dry before pulling on pyjama bottoms and rummaging through her closet for a nightshirt. It was easy to slip the nightie over her head, and it felt natural to sit on the bed and cradle her in his arms.

For a moment, he said nothing but simply buried his face in her newly shampooed hair, revelling at the feel of her in his arms. Mma hadn't uttered a word at all, except when she had said a soft "thank you" in the shower.

Now she sat down in his arms quietly, saying nothing, just waiting for him to speak.

"I love you."

When he finally spoke, his voice was soft. She wasn't sure she heard him correctly. She said nothing, averting her gaze and willing him to repeat it, say it louder.

He did. He took hold of her chin so that she had no other option but to meet his gaze. His heart broke when he saw her eyes shining with unshed tears.

"I love you," he repeated, saying the words she had been waiting to hear. Her heart soared with joy as she reached out to touch his lips.

"I know." She nodded.

With a groan, Fuad cradled her face in his hands as he kissed her hard. "I'm so sorry, Mma," he moaned when he finally broke the kiss. "I'm sorry, my love, forgive me?"

And that was when the dam broke. All the pain, all the hurt she felt came rushing back.

Mma burst into tears.

"I thought you were regretting getting married to me. You changed so much towards me after I told you how I felt," she said in between sobs as Fuad cradled her in his arms, rocking back and forth on the bed.

"I'm so sorry, my love, I really am. Marrying you was the best thing that happened to me. We connected. I had never felt that way about a woman before I met you. I liked and respected you and was sure I would grow to love you. I was already half in love with you by the time we went to Italy for our honeymoon, but when you told me you loved me, I freaked out. I didn't know how to handle your love. Sex, I can deal with, it's practical, I can control it, but love. It just consumes you. I was so scared." He kissed her eyelids, her nose, her lips. "Please stop crying, Mma" He kissed her again. "Please, it breaks me to see you cry."

Mma nodded, trying to control her sobs. "You moved out of our room again."

"I'm an idiot," He grinned ruefully, wiping away her tears with the pad of his thumbs. "While you lay in bed in a coma, I thought I would die if you didn't make it. I had no idea if you would come back to me. I spent the whole one week you were in a coma imagining what I would say if you woke up. When you did, I couldn't talk. The words wouldn't come out, and I just froze. I even refused to see Fa'izah for fear that I would blame her. Mma, you complete me. You are my heart; you inspire me, and I don't regret marrying you."

He pulled back to look down at her.

"I miss holding you. I miss waking up beside you, with you in my arms. I miss our fights, our chats, our lovemaking. I miss everything about you. I love you, babe," he whispered, "I need you to believe me." He grinned. "I went out and bought you Glover Court suya."

She burst into laughter, pulling his head down to kiss his cheek.

"I need you to believe me, babe," he repeated when she had stopped laughing.

"I do. I was just waiting for you to say it," she whispered as she pulled his head down again for a kiss.

Fuad kissed her. He worshipped her, apologised, and spoke of his love, all in one kiss.

"I love you, Fuad," his wife whispered as he rained kisses on her face.

"Forever, babe," Fuad replied. Lifting her, he placed her on the bed, then came down to lie by her.

He looked down into her face and smiled.

"I love you forever and a day," he said, and he kissed her again.

Mma kissed him back, revelling, and secure in the knowledge that he loved her. How had she ever doubted that? With him, she was free to be herself. Free to reveal everything about her—her secrets, desires, soul, and heart.

Fuad was her other half. He completed her.

"Fuad," she breathed as his hands slid under her nightshirt to trace the jagged scars on her upper thigh. He slid down and kissed the welts on her thighs, her legs, her stomach, then he moved back up to look into her eyes, his hands cradling her face.

"I'm here, Mma, always." And he was.

And then he made her pay, in the delicious way only he could. The way he always did, the way he loved her and worshipped her, brought tears to her eyes.

Mma knew she would be fine.

They would be okay. Because underneath everything, their love was real.

EPILOGUE

One year later, Fuad and Mma went to Italy.

Mma's mum moved into their house to look after Fa'izah so they could take two weeks off. Her healing process hadn't been easy. But Fuad had been there, holding her hand every step of the way, coaxing her, encouraging her when she wanted to give up.

Six months of intense physiotherapy, but it had been worth it. She was still limping and walking with aid. She still had a long way to go before her leg would heal fully, Dr Okon had told her on her last visit to the hospital.

They stayed at their favourite hotel, Le Sirenuse, Albergo di Positano. Fuad was happy that she was getting better, and he had been so excited to book a two-week holiday in Italy.

Smiling at the bellhop who brought their luggage into their suite, she walked into the room, her cane tapping against the marble flooring.

After the hotel staff left, he scooped her into his arms and placed her on the sofa in the suite. "How are you feeling? The trip was long,"

"I'm feeling great. I need this holiday. I miss Fa'izah, but I'm glad that we have this time together" She smiled, linking her arms around his neck to pull his head down for a kiss.

"Me too," Fuad whispered, kissing her back on the lips.

***

The next day, he took her on a private boat tour from Positano. Her squeal of delight when she saw that they were going on a private tour sailing along the UNESCO-listed coastline made him smile.

She turned in delight. "Another boat tour! I love it. Where are we going to?"

He grinned, curving an arm around her to draw her closer. "I thought maybe we could spend the night in Sorrento. In the same hotel we stayed last time and maybe...."

"Maybe what?" Mma asked, her eyebrows raised as she watched a mischievous grin split her husband's face.

"Maybe, give Fa'izah a brother or two!" he replied, bursting into laughter when she poked him in the ribs.

"You are such a bad boy, Fuad!" She teased, laughing. "But I love you like that!"

"Yes, I am, but I am your bad boy, and I love you more," he replied, just before he kissed her.

THE END

ABOUT THE AUTHOR

OMO OBONNA was born in Lagos, Nigeria. She holds degrees in Creative Arts/English and Supply Chain Management. For as long as she can remember, she always wanted to tell stories about love and romance by creating and immersing readers in the romantic adventures of fascinating characters.

Her stories are a peek into her own version of the excitement, allure, and mystery of the age-old sentimental narrative of love, which she so beautifully and intricately weaves together into a truly engrossing read. When she's not surrounding herself with words or reading a romance novel, you can find her in the kitchen trying out new recipes or painting with her children. In addition, she enjoys writing and recently joined the worlds of bloggers.

She lives in London and is happily married with three children.

Connect with Omo
Instagram: https://www.instagram.com/omos_corner/
Twitter - https://twitter.com/omoscorner
Facebook: https://www.facebook.com/omoscorner/
Web: www.omoscorner.com

OTHER BOOKS BY LOVE AFRICA PRESS

Love on a Mission by Jomi Oyel

Note Worthy by Dhasi Mwale

The Torn Prince by Zee Monodee

The Tainted Prince by Kiru Taye

CONNECT WITH US

Facebook.com/LoveAfricaPress

Twitter.com/LoveAfricaPress

Instagram.com/LoveAfricaPress

www.loveafricapress.com

Printed in Great Britain
by Amazon